**She watched his hands on the reins. His skin was tanned, his fingers long and capable-looking.**

Winifred was in awe of this man. And she liked sitting close to him.

She edged toward him a few inches and laid her head against his shoulder. No one would see them; they had not yet reached the road back to town.

Zane made a sound in his throat, pulled the horse to a stop and wound the reins around the brake handle. He turned to her, his gray eyes dark and smoky. He caught her mouth under his, moving his lips over hers slowly, purposefully. She wanted it to go on forever.

He deepened the kiss and she opened her lips. He tasted of lemons and something sweet, and all at once she wanted to weep.

She touched his arms, felt the muscles bunch and tremble. She ached for something more, something... closer.

"Zane," she murmured against his mouth. "Touch me."

## Author Note

It wasn't always easy to face the realities of life in the Old West, especially when it came to loss and pain. And when it came to falling in love again, matters could get extremely complicated.

I hope you will enjoy this story of heartache and hope.

# LYNNA BANNING

## SMOKE RIVER FAMILY

**HARLEQUIN**®HISTORICAL

Recycling programs
for this product may
not exist in your area.

ISBN-13: 978-0-373-29856-3

Smoke River Family

Copyright © 2015 by The Woolston Family Trust

This is a work of fiction. Names, characters, places and incidents are either the product of the author's imagination or are used fictitiously, and any resemblance to actual persons, living or dead, business establishments, events or locales is entirely coincidental.

This edition published by arrangement with Harlequin Books S.A.

For questions and comments about the quality of this book, please contact us at CustomerService@Harlequin.com.

® and TM are trademarks of Harlequin Enterprises Limited or its corporate affiliates. Trademarks indicated with ® are registered in the United States Patent and Trademark Office, the Canadian Intellectual Property Office and in other countries.

**Printed in U.S.A.**

**Lynna Banning** combines a lifelong love of history and literature into a satisfying career as a writer. Born in Oregon, she graduated from Scripps College and embarked on a career as an editor and technical writer and later as a high school English teacher. She enjoys hearing from her readers. You may write to her directly at PO Box 324, Felton, CA 95018, USA, email her at carowoolston@att.net or visit Lynna's website at lynnabanning.net.

### Books by Lynna Banning

### Harlequin Historical

Visit the Author Profile page at Harlequin.com for more titles.

For my agent, Pattie Steele-Perkins

# Chapter One

Smoke River, Oregon
August 1871

The train chuffed to a stop and Winifred peered out at the town. A seedy-looking building with two large dust-covered windows faced the station; Smoke River Hotel was emblazoned across the front in foot-high dirty white printed lettering. Winifred groaned at the sight. The thought of two whole weeks in this rough Western town made her stomach tighten.

"End of the line, miss," the conductor bawled.

She blew out a shaky breath and straightened her spine. Most definitely the end of the line. Where else on God's earth would one see such an array of ramshackle structures leaning into the wind? Could Cissy really have been happy in such a place?

The passenger car door thumped open. "Ya might wanna catch yer breath a minute when you get to the station. Heat can get to ya, ya know."

No, she did not know. She eyed the purple-hazed mountains in the distance. St. Louis was flat as a sadiron and the downtown area was extremely well kept. She had no idea Oregon would be so…well, scruffy.

She twitched the dirt from her forest green travel skirt and set one foot onto the iron step. The conductor, a short, squat butterball of a man, extended a callused hand.

"Watch yer step, now. Can't have any passenger fallin' on her—" He coughed and cleared his throat. Winifred noted his cheeks had turned red. She grasped his outstretched hand and stepped onto the ground.

Her head felt funny, as if her brain were stuffed with wet cotton. Her ears rang. She released the conductor's hand and took a single step, then grabbed the man's beefy hand again.

"Dizzy, are ya?" He steadied her arm and peered into her face. "Happens all the time. Folks don't notice the climb on the train, but the el'vation rises up little by little and then, *kapow*! With this heat, feels like dynamite's exploded inside yer body."

It felt, she thought, like stage fright, only her hands didn't shake.

"Ya wanna set a spell at the station house while I get somebody to tote yer portmantle?"

*Portmanteau*, she corrected automatically. "N-no, I am quite all right." She took three unsteady steps and stopped.

"Hard to breathe, ain't it? Kinda hot today."

*Hot*? The air seemed to smother her every breath, as if she were trapped inside a bell jar. She struggled for oxygen, opening her mouth like a hungry goldfish. It didn't help that her corset was laced too tight.

"Where d'ya want yer luggage toted, miss?"

"Dr. Dougherty's residence." She panted for a moment, fighting the whirly sensation in her brain. "Dr. Nathaniel Dougherty." She swallowed hard to keep inside the bitter words she'd like to level at the man.

"Right. Top of the hill, past the new hospital, 'bout six blocks. Ya sure you're all right?"

"I will be quite all right in a moment." She could see the large white house at the end of the main street. It looked to be at least a mile away, and straight up a mountainside.

"Suit yerself, miss." The conductor stepped past her.

"Charlie," he yelled to a gray-bearded man lounging on the station house bench. "Carry this lady's bag up to Doc Dougherty's, will ya?"

The man nodded, hefted her travel bag onto his rounded shoulder and set off at a fast clip. She took a step in the same direction. Oh, my. Could she really walk that far with her head reeling like this?

She followed the man up the hill, trying not to totter even though she felt disturbingly unsteady. She would *not* arrive at Dr. Dougherty's doorstep shaking and out of breath. She would need all her wits about her.

She plodded up past the new-looking two-story building. Samuel Graham Hospital, the sign said. That was where Cissy...

She swallowed hard.

The last fifty yards up the hill she slowed to conserve her energy and met the man—Charlie— tramping back down.

"I put yer portmantle on the doc's porch," he said jauntily. "Good luck to ya, miss. He's home, so I'm bettin' ye'll need it."

An odd juxtaposition, Winifred thought. Why would she need luck because Dr. Dougherty was at home? The doctor must be extremely bad-tempered.

The lawn swing on the wide front porch beck-oned, but to reach it she had to climb five—no, six steps. She paused before the first step to catch her breath. Then she managed one-two-three-four—

and... She halted at the fifth step, panting, then heaved herself up onto the sixth.

Such thin air was surely not good for a baby. Especially a newborn. She propelled herself up onto the porch and sank down in the swing.

Zane laid his fingertips on either side of the bridge of his nose and pressed hard. The headache throbbed behind his eyes and deep within both temples, and he shut his eyes against the relentless pain. It came upon him every afternoon ever since Celeste—he could not finish the thought. He gulped the half glass of whiskey at his elbow and bent his head. *God in heaven, help me.*

He refilled the glass and sat staring at his shaking hand as it replaced the stopper on the cut glass decanter. He could see the veins, the tendons of each finger, but it was as if the hand no longer belonged to him.

Never again would he pat a bereaved husband or wife on the shoulder and reassure them their grief would pass. He knew better now; grief did not pass. It would never pass.

He sipped from his glass and bowed his head again.

Winifred heaved herself out of the swing and stepped unsteadily to the glass-paneled front door.

Hung to one side on a metal arm was an old ship's bell with a clapper of tarnished copper. She winced at the sound it made, raucous as a hungry crow.

The door swung open and a young Oriental man looked at her inquiringly. She took a breath to steady her voice. "Is this Dr. Nathaniel Dougherty's residence?"

The houseboy gave a quick nod. "Yes, missy. But too late for appointment."

"I do not wish to make an appointment. I wish to speak to the doctor."

"Come in, please, missy." He gestured her inside and closed the door behind her. "You sick?"

"No, I..." Her breath ran out before she could finish explaining. "I..." Her vision went watery and black spots swam before her eyes. In the next instant the floor rushed up to meet her.

"Boss!" Wing Sam yelled. "Come quick! Lady has fainted."

Zane thrust open his office door to see Sam on his knees beside a young woman. "Get my smelling salts," he ordered.

He knelt and bent over the motionless form, slipped free half the buttons down the front of her dress, then searched for her corset lacings. Sam thrust the lavender salts into his grasp and he uncapped the bottle and waved it under her nose.

The woman twisted her head away and batted

feebly at his hands as he was unlacing her stays. "Stop that!" Her voice was unsteady, but the intent was clear.

His hands stilled. "I'm sorry, miss, but you fainted in my hallway. I am trying to aid your breathing."

She opened her eyes and his heart jolted against his ribs. My God, they were the same clear blue-green as Celeste's. The unexpected rush of pain was like a knife blade.

He pressed two fingers on her wrist. Pulse fast but irregular. Heat exhaustion, probably. Wouldn't be the first time a woman had succumbed to a too-snug corset. Why *did* young women persist in such foolishness?

"Help me sit her up, Sam." Together they raised her shoulders. Her lids drifted closed and he gave her another whiff of smelling salts.

"Miss? Take a deep breath, now. It's only the heat, I think," he said to Sam. "Must be a flat-lander."

"Pretty lady," Sam observed.

Zane hadn't noticed. He watched the young woman slowly regain consciousness again. She jerked when she realized her front buttons were undone.

"I undid them," he reminded her. "To loosen your corset."

"You must be Dr. Dougherty," she said slowly.

"That I am."

"Dr. Nathaniel Dougherty?"

She was fully awake now. He watched those not green, not blue eyes focus on his face.

"Yes. And you are...?"

She drew in a long breath and expelled it, all the while scrabbling to close her front buttons. "Do you always undress your visitors?"

"As I said, I undid them to— Answer my question, please. Who are you? Are you ill?"

"I am not ill. At least I wasn't when I arrived at the train station. I am Winifred Von Dannen. Celeste's sister."

Zane sat back on his heels and stared at her. Of course. Same pale skin and high cheekbones, the same determined chin, the same... He found he couldn't look into those eyes.

Something ripped inside his chest. "I see." Dammit, his voice shook. "I would welcome you to my home, Miss Von Dannen, but you are lying flat on my floor."

"I must get up," she said in a decisive tone. "This is most undignified."

Sam took the vial of salts from his hand and Zane helped the woman sit fully upright. Then he clasped both her elbows and lifted her to her feet.

"Thank you," she breathed. She gazed at him and waited.

"I—forgive me, you were not expected so soon."

"Did you not receive my telegram from St. Louis?"

"Yes, I—" He had read it three times but he could not remember what it said.

"I left earlier than I had planned. I wanted to…" Her eyes looked shiny. "I wanted to see Celeste's grave. And the baby. I came to see the baby."

"Of course." He had not been able to revisit his wife's grave site. After watching them lower the coffin into that dark hole that day, he doubted he would ever be able to visit. The pain behind his eyes throbbed.

"This is most awkward," she said. "If you do not mind, I need to sit down."

He guided her to one of the straight-backed chairs in the wide hallway that served as his waiting room. "Sam, bring some tea."

"No, please. I am quite all right now."

He tipped up her chin and peered into her chalk-white face. "And some sandwiches," he called. "You look half-famished, Miss Von Dannen."

"Yes, I am, now that I think about it. I was in such a hurry to get here, you see."

Zane nodded. He did not see. She had not come

for the funeral; the wire he'd received had explained she was away on tour. Still, she must be
anxious to see the baby.

Sam appeared with a tray of tea and a plate of
tiny sandwiches, the kind he served when Zane
skipped too many meals or spent too many long
hours at the hospital.

"Come into the dining room, Miss Von Dannen." Zane guided her to an upholstered chair at
one end of the carved walnut table. She fell on the
sandwiches at once and he poured the aromatic
tea into the blue china cups. Sam had used the
good china, he noted. It reminded him of when
Celeste— His hand shook, and he clattered his
own cup back onto the saucer.

She ate in silence, and he sipped his tea and
watched her. Couldn't help watching her, in fact.
She was a bit older than Celeste, more settled
somehow. Less excitable. Then he remembered
that Winifred Von Dannen was a professor of
music in St. Louis, at the same academy where
Celeste had studied. Of course, someone of her
stature would not be young, at least not as young
as his wife had been. In fact, Winifred Von Dannen was well-known in the East. A pianist, like
Celeste.

"I was more hungry than I thought," she said.
She replaced her cup on the blue-flowered saucer

and looked up, straight into his eyes. The ripping inside his chest tore at him. She looked so much like Celeste.

"Now," she said. "May I see the baby?"

## Chapter Two

The doctor paused outside one doorway in the spacious upstairs hall, laid one hand on the brass knob and hesitated. Winifred waited. Did he have some intimation of why she was really here?

"I think she is asleep," he said softly. "At least for the moment."

"Oh?" Winifred knew absolutely nothing about babies.

"She rarely sleeps through the night," the doctor explained.

Ah. That would explain the dark circles beneath his tired gray eyes. He looked as if he had not slept in weeks. Months, perhaps. But of course there was his grief, too.

For a moment her throat grew tight. She had been in Europe when she had heard the news of her sister's death. She had cried and cried for weeks.

But a man losing his wife…she could scarcely imagine such anguish. Even for a man she detested.

The doctor quietly opened the door and preceded her into a warm, comfortable room with a large bed and a paper-strewn desk under the window. *Oh! This must be his bedroom.*

Next to the quilt-covered bed stood a white wicker bassinet on wheels. He gestured toward it. "She sleeps in here so I can hear her when she cries at night," he said. "She likes to be rocked."

Holding her breath, Winifred tiptoed forward. A tiny face peeked out from the pink flannel blanket, her eyes wide open. Blue-green, just like her own and Cissy's. Winifred's heart did something odd, and a clenching feeling under her breastbone left her short of breath.

"She's so beautiful," she murmured. Tears stung her eyes.

"Yes." He smoothed a long, slim forefinger against the pink-and-white skin of the baby's cheek. "Her name is Rosemarie."

"Rosemarie," she breathed. After their mother.

"Rosemarie… Winifred," he added after a slight hesitation.

Winifred's tears spilled over. "Cissy named her after me? Really?"

"Of course," the doctor said. "I would not lie

when it comes to my daughter. It was Celeste's last wish."

Oh, God. Oh, Cissy. *Cissy.* For a moment she could not speak.

"Would you like to hold your niece?" He reached into the bassinet, lifted out the pink bundle and offered the baby to her.

"Oh, no. I mean, yes, I would. But—but I really don't know how to—I mean, I know very little about handling babies."

The doctor gave her a long look, then laid Rosemarie into her arms. "You can learn."

Winifred looked down into the blue-green eyes. "Can she really see me?"

"Probably not, at least not clearly. But if you talk to her, she will hear your voice."

"Oh." How did one talk to a baby? All at once she felt awkward and out of place and ignorant of the most basic things of life. All she knew about was music and teaching.

"Go on," he urged in a quiet voice. "Try it."

Winifred inhaled and exhaled twice, working up her courage. She felt as fluttery as on the opening night of a concert, excited and terrified and thrilled at the same time.

"H-hello, Rosemarie. My, you are so beautiful. You look like Cissy, did you know that?"

"Cissy?" the doctor murmured.

"Celeste. I call—called her Cissy. She called me Freddie."

"That I would never have guessed. She always referred to you as Winifred."

A tiny fist waved toward Winifred's hand. She extended her forefinger and the baby latched onto it. "Oh, just look," she whispered.

"She likes fingers," the doctor said, a hint of a smile in his voice. "Thumbs, especially."

Winifred could not speak. The small hand, the knuckles wrinkled and rosy, the tiny fingernails so perfect, kept its grip on Winifred's finger. Her senses swirled again; she must still be dizzy from the altitude.

"Shall I take her?" the doctor asked.

"No, I— Could we wait until she releases my finger?"

He laughed softly and nodded, watching her.

"Rosemarie," she breathed. "I am your aunt Fred—your aunt Winifred. And you are my only, most precious, most beautiful niece."

The little mouth opened and a soft cry came out.

"She's hungry," the doctor said. He walked to the door and opened it. "Sam?"

In three heartbeats, the houseboy appeared, a glass bottle of milk in one hand and a towel in the other. Expertly he lifted the baby out of Winifred's arms and cradled her in his own. Then he

began walking up and down in front of the cur-
tained window, crooning something in a strange
language while Rosemarie gulped milk through
the rubber nipple.

"Does he—Sam—have children of his own?"
Winifred asked quietly.

"Sam? Sam is not married. Not many Chinese
women are admitted into this country. And an
American woman would not be acceptable. The
Chinese are proud that way, they wish to preserve
their heritage."

Winifred's eyes rested on the Chinese man's
slim form. "How sad that must be."

The doctor did not answer. Instead, he gestured
her into the hallway and quietly closed the door.
"The guest bedroom is next door. Sam has already
brought up your travel case."

He opened another door into an airy room with
pretty yellow curtains and a crocheted yellow coverlet on the bed.

"Would you like to rest awhile? Sam will call
you when supper is ready."

"Yes, I suppose I should. I feel quite shaky
after my travels." After meeting Rosemarie, she
amended. That had been the biggest shock of her
life. Well, perhaps the second biggest. The biggest
surprise had been when Cissy had eloped with Dr.
Nathaniel Dougherty and ruined everything.

\* \* \*

That evening, Winifred entered the dining room determined to discuss her plan with Dr. Dougherty. Instead, she found herself alone at the huge walnut table. Sam had tapped on her bedroom door twenty minutes earlier to announce supper, and she had roused herself from an exhausted sleep, rebraided her hair and donned her travel skirt and a fresh shirtwaist. As she descended the staircase she rehearsed what she had come to say.

She acknowledged a distinct nervous flutter in the pit of her stomach. She also admitted she felt torn between dislike and an unexpected attraction to the tall, square-jawed physician. She resented the man. And feared him. Would he stand in her way when she confessed her purpose?

Sam stepped into the dining room. "Missy like glass of wine?"

"Not now, thank you. I will wait for the doctor."

"Doctor not come," Sam replied.

"Oh? Why not?"

"Go to hospital. Wife of sheriff having twins." He grinned at her, revealing straight white teeth and an unexpected dimple in one cheek.

Disappointment swept over her. She had worked up her courage to speak with him; now the matter would have to wait.

"You like fish, missy? Catch fresh from river

and cook quick." Sam waited, his hands folded together at the waist of his blue knee-length tunic. "Or I cook chicken, very nice fat hen."

Winifred nodded. "Chicken, please." She wasn't the least bit hungry. In fact, her head still ached, but she knew she must eat to keep up her resolve. She could not argue her case on an empty stomach.

"I go cook chicken." The houseboy bobbed his head and turned away.

"Sam, wait. When do you expect the doctor?"

"Not know. Sometimes baby take long time."

"What about Rosemarie?"

"Sam take good care of baby. Feed, rock, change and more feed." He grinned again. "I good mother."

Winifred bit her lip. No one but a real mother was a good mother, she thought. She and Cissy had known that from the time her sister was barely out of diapers. That was why—never mind. Her head hurt too much to think about it now.

After her meal of succulent chicken breast and wonderfully flavored green peas and rice, she retired to her room, listening for the doctor's step in the hallway. Sam brought up hot tea for her headache, and the last thing she remembered before falling asleep was his queer crooning from the next room as he walked up and down with the baby.

The next morning when she came down for

breakfast, the doctor was already seated at the table.

"Good morning," she offered. She slid onto her chair, then glanced at the man sitting opposite her. His face was chalk-white with fatigue. Dark stubble masked the lower part of his chin and dark circles shadowed the skin beneath his eyes. His once-white shirt was rumpled and open at the neck, the sleeves rolled up to his elbows.

He gazed at her with unfocused gray eyes as Sam bustled in with a pot of coffee. The doctor stirred three spoons of sugar into his cup while the houseboy poured Winifred's cup full. She lifted the brew to her lips. *Now. I must speak to him now.*

But he looked so completely spent she hesitated. He was in no state to hear her out.

Sam tapped the doctor's shoulder. "Boss want eggs now?"

He dropped his head into a loose-necked nod.

"Missy?"

Winifred stared at the man across the table from her. It was obvious he was only half-awake.

"Missy, you like eggs?"

"What? Oh, yes, thank you." She turned toward the Chinese man for an instant, then swung her gaze back to the doctor. His head was tipped back against the high ladder-back chair, his eyes closed, his breathing slow and even. Good Lord, the man was sound asleep!

"Up all night," Sam murmured. "Babies come slow." He moved the coffee cup away from the doctor's hand and tiptoed into the kitchen.

Winifred stared at Nathaniel Dougherty. She could not tell him what she had come all the way from St. Louis to say. Not while he was this tired.

In a few moments, Sam slid a plate of scrambled eggs in front of her, motioned for her to eat, then laid one long finger across his lips to signal silence. She nodded, picked up her fork and quietly devoured the perfectly cooked eggs.

She studied the plate of toast at her elbow and lifted a slice to her mouth but could not bring herself to take a single bite. The crunching sound might wake him.

He slept on, his breathing guttural, his chest rising and falling. Winifred drank her coffee in silence and watched him. Her throat felt tight each time she swallowed.

A faint wail floated from the floor above and suddenly the doctor jerked awake and bolted for the stairway.

Sam shot into the dining room and shook his head at the empty chair. "I feed baby. Doctor must sleep." On silent black slippers he padded up the stairs after the doctor.

Winifred couldn't help smiling at the house-boy's retreating back. Sam was obviously devoted to Dr. Dougherty. Perhaps he had also been devoted to Cissy. As for the doctor...

Well, she had to admit she had been prepared not to like Nathaniel Dougherty. But since breakfast, a tiny niggle of doubt had lodged in her brain.

"Missy like read book?"

Sam's voice brought her bolt upright, and her coffee cup clanked onto the saucer.

The houseboy's black eyes snapped with delight. "Baby sleep. Doctor sleep. Maybe you read book? We have library."

"Why, yes." She needed something to do with herself until she could speak with Rosemarie's father. A book was just the answer.

"You come see book room," Sam invited. "Fine books. You come. Bring coffee."

Winifred followed him through the wide entry hall and past a set of sliding pocket doors into a large parlor lined with floor-to-ceiling bookshelves. Sam swept one arm in an expansive circle. "Here many fine books. You choose."

But she had spied the dark cherrywood grand piano in the corner and her breath stopped. Cissy's piano! She had forgotten how beautiful the instrument was, the wood polished to a gleaming burgundy color, the upholstered bench carved to match the ornate piano legs. It looked untouched, as if Cissy had just finished playing and left the room only a moment before. Her eyes filled with tears.

"Doctor's favorite books here, lady's books there." Sam pointed to the shelf behind the piano.

Cissy's music books. Mostly familiar worn volumes—Brahms. Mozart. Beethoven. The corners of some pages were turned down. The ache in her heart flared into rage. *How could she? How had she dared?*

Winifred set the cup and saucer on a side table and began to thumb through the Brahms as Sam glided away. Yes, the waltzes, the intermezzos they both loved, all arranged for four hands.

Abruptly she slapped the volume shut. Oh, Cissy. *Cissy.*

She couldn't look at the music any longer. Instead she moved to the doctor's book collection and ran her hand over the leather-bound volumes. She selected a volume of Wordsworth. Next to it, Milton's *Paradise Lost* caught her eye. "How prophetic," she murmured. A stab of bitterness knifed through her.

*We had it all, Cissy, everything we had dreamed of. And you threw it away for this man. Why?*

She fled into the hallway. "Sam?" she called. "I am going out for a walk."

She heard no answer, but it didn't matter. She

opened the front door and the heat hit her like a fist. Just as she was about to give up the idea, Sam appeared with a wide-brimmed straw hat in one hand. Cissy's hat. A wide pink ribbon banded the crown, and her heart caught. Winifred never wore pink. The Chinese man offered it without a word.

She tied it beneath her chin and stepped out onto the porch, then resolutely marched down the front steps, past the hospital and on down the tree-lined street toward town.

It wasn't much of a main street. A single mercantile with bushel baskets of apples and squash out in front; the Smoke River sheriff's office; a scruffy-looking barber shop; Uncle Charlie's bakery, with a large, many-paned window through which she glimpsed a glass case of cakes and cookies.

Next door to the bakery hung a sign with large block letters printed in royal blue: Verena Forester, Dressmaker. A handsome challis morning dress was displayed in the window, and she hesitated. But no. She did not plan to be here long enough to warrant adding to her wardrobe.

By the time she reached the Smoke River Hotel, she was wilting and dizzy from the heat. A young man with a silver badge on his plaid shirt glanced at her as she passed, then doubled back and fell into step beside her.

"You all right, ma'am? Look kinda, well, peaked. I thought maybe you'd—"

"I am quite all right. Just a bit… Is it always this hot here in the summer?"

"Usually much worse. Oh, 'scuse me, ma'am." He tipped his hat. "I'm Sandy Boggs, the deputy sheriff. Sheriff's at the hospital with his wife. Had twins this morning. Kin I escort you some place?"

She nodded. "A place with cold lemonade, perhaps?"

"That'd be right here, ma'am. Restaurant's next to the hotel." He tipped his hat again and strode off down the street.

Inside the restaurant Winifred sank down at a table and fanned herself with Cissy's hat. Without even asking, the waitress brought a large glass of cold water and plunked it at her elbow.

"Must be from somewheres else, I'd guess," the plump woman said. "Otherwise you'd be used to it. The heat, I mean."

"St. Louis," Winifred volunteered. "Would you have any lemonade?"

"Got gallons of it, ma'am. 'Spect we'll need to make another batch or two before noon. Never been this hot in August." The woman whipped a pad and pencil from her checked apron pocket. "You want anything else?"

*Oh, yes. She wanted a great deal.* "No, thank you. Wait! Where is the cemetery?"

"The graveyard, ya mean? Top of the hill." She gestured a thick arm in the opposite direction from the doctor's house.

Winifred drank two glasses of excellent cold lemonade, then donned her hat and started up the other hill. Thank goodness she hadn't laced her corset tight this morning. She didn't fancy fainting twice in Dr. Dougherty's entrance hall.

At the top of the rise she spied a neatly fenced area with leafy green trees and chiseled headstones. A spreading oak shaded the area, and she sank down on the thick grass beneath it to catch her breath.

At the sight of the mound of fresh dirt indicating a recent burial, she closed her eyes tight and began to cry. She thought she would be over these bouts of weeping she'd fought this past month; perhaps she would never get over Cissy's death.

Maybe not, but now there was Rosemarie. And, she acknowledged, swiping tears off her cheeks, Rosemarie was the reason she had come.

## Chapter Three

A handful of yellow roses lay on top of Cissy's grave. Winifred's heart squeezed at the sight. Dr. Dougherty must have paid an early-morning visit after delivering the sheriff's twins. She swallowed a hiccupped sob. Even in death, her sister was fortunate.

She still resented Nathaniel Dougherty's sweeping Cissy off to this rough, uncivilized place, but a small part of her ached at the man's obvious sorrow. She knew how devastating it was to lose someone you loved; it must be doubly so if you had pledged to share your life with that person.

She sank down beside the grave site and struggled to compose her thoughts. *You knew I would come, didn't you, Cissy? Was your husband so crushed by your loss that he could not tell me of your death until after the funeral?*

She yanked up shoots of the green grass poking up from the earth beside her and crushed them in her palm. *I would have come, Cissy. You know I would.*

She removed the straw hat and bowed her head. The angle of the sun shifted and she felt its rays warm her shoulders and then burn slowly through the light muslin shirtwaist she wore. She did not care. She rolled the sleeves up to her elbows and stayed where she was beside her sister's grave.

She tried to stop feeling, stop thinking. Instead, she steadily shredded the grass under her hand and stared at those yellow roses. They were beginning to wilt in the sunshine.

Suddenly a chill swept through her. How strange loss could be. When Mama was killed, Papa straightened his shoulders and went back to his desk at the bank. He had provided for Cissy and herself, sent them to private schools and later to the music conservatory. They had maids and cooks and tutors, but the hole in their hearts yawned like a chasm. Papa bore it best. He never wept, as she and Cissy had.

Remembering those black days, she turned her face up to the sun and lost track of time.

"Ah, glad you back, missy. Doctor go see boy who have chicken spots."

"You mean chicken pox?"

"Ah. 'Pox,'" he pronounced carefully. "Learn new English word. Make stew for your supper. Tonight I play fan-tan with friend Ming Cha. You stay here with baby?"

"Me? But I know noth—"

"Not hard, missy. I show."

Sam demonstrated how to heat the nippled bottle of milk and sprinkle some on her wrist to check the temperature, and then, with a wide grin that showed his elusive dimple, he was gone.

Oh, well. How hard could it be to feed a month-old baby?

Besides, she must learn these things if she wanted to bring her plan to fruition.

She dawdled over her stew and the fluffy dumpling Sam had added, listening for Rosemarie's hungry cry from upstairs and praying desperately for the doctor's return.

But Dr. Dougherty did not return. When Rosemarie's faint wail rose, Winifred heated the milk as Sam had shown her and flew up the stairs to feed her precious niece. By the time she opened the door to the doctor's bedroom where the baby lay in the ruffled wicker bassinet, Rosemarie had worked up to quite a lusty yell.

"There, there, little one," Winifred crooned. She set the warmed milk on the book-cluttered nightstand and lifted the child into her arms. A sopping wet diaper plastered itself against the front of her shirtwaist and instantly she held the baby away from her. Oh, dear. She would have to exchange the wet garment for a dry one; but how, exactly, did one accomplish this? Sam had left no instructions concerning wet diapers.

She riffled through the handsome walnut chest of drawers until she found clean diapers, then laid Rosemarie on the doctor's bed and studied how the safety pins were arranged. Rosemarie screamed and grew red in the face, and Winifred began to perspire.

She unpinned the soaked garment, prodded the ceramic chamber pot out from under the bassinet with her foot and dropped in the diaper. It landed with a splat and Winifred heaved a sigh of relief. Then she pinned the dry garment onto the now-squirming infant, praying she would not prick the soft skin. Then she stuck the rubber nipple into Rosemarie's open mouth.

Instant silence. Thank the Lord! The blue-green eyes popped open and gazed into Winifred's face as the level of milk in the bottle steadily diminished. The baby sucked greedily while she hovered over her, mesmerized by the whole process. Perhaps it wasn't that difficult to care for an infant.

Long before the bottle was empty, Rosemarie fell asleep. Winifred cuddled her against one shoulder and settled into the rocking chair by the window. Not difficult at all, she mused. In fact, she felt exactly like she did after a successful concert—tired and proud and happy.

Zane stepped quietly into his bedroom and stopped short. Winifred sat in the rocker, asleep, with a slumbering Rosemarie nestled against her shoulder. Very gently he lifted his daughter into his arms, felt her diaper—dry—and laid her in the bassinet beside his bed. Then he stood staring down at Celeste's sister.

How different this woman was from his wife. Celeste had been petite, golden-blonde and frail-looking. Winifred had dark hair. And whereas Celeste had been slim to the point of boyishness, Winifred's breasts under the white shirtwaist were lushly curved.

She slept quietly, her breath pulling softly in and out without a hint of the asthma that had plagued Celeste in the summer months. His wife had been pretty, extremely pretty; but Winifred's bone structure approached real beauty. He could not help wondering how far the differences between the two sisters went. Was Winifred—? He caught himself. He wouldn't allow his mind to go there. He recognized that he was desperately unhappy. Lonely. Hungry, even. Not for physical release but for emotional comfort. And, yes, he supposed, some plain old body hunger was involved. It amazed him that his spirit could feel so broken and his physical self could still feel normal. Or almost normal.

Since Celeste's death he hadn't felt a twinge of interest in food or riding or swimming or reading or any of the things that had sustained him through the long, dry months of her pregnancy. He supposed he would come back to life eventually; for the time being, it was a blessing to feel nothing.

He reached out and touched Winifred's wrist and she jerked upright with a little cry. "Oh, it's you."

Zane surprised himself with a chuckle. "Who were you expecting?"

She surged out of the rocker. "The baby! Where is—?"

"Sleeping," Zane replied.

She took a single step forward and her knees gave way. Zane snagged one arm around her shoulder to steady her. "Easy, there. Foot go to sleep?"

"What? Oh, no, I…" She swerved toward the bassinet. "I feel somewhat unsteady, and my head is pounding like it does when I have a migraine."

Zane tightened his grip and steered her through the doorway and down the short hallway to the guest bedroom. Her skin was hot. Even through the shirtwaist he could feel she was over-warm. He shot a glance to her flushed face.

"Winifred, undress and get into bed. I'll bring up something to cool you down."

When he returned, she was stretched out under the top sheet, her eyes shut. "What's wrong with me? Am I ill?"

"You're sun-sick. Got a bad sunburn on your face and arms. Here, drink this." He leaned over, slipped his arm behind her to raise her shoulders and held a glass to her lips.

"What is it?"

"Water, mostly. You're dehydrated. What did you do today to get this sunburned?"

She sipped obligingly, then grasped the glass with both hands and gulped down four huge swallows. "I went to visit Cissy's grave. I must have sat there for longer than I thought."

Zane said nothing. Her next statement drove the breath from his lungs.

"I saw your roses. It was a lovely gesture."

"What roses?"

"The yellow ones you left on her grave."

"But I did not—"

Even in the semidarkness he could see her eyes widen. She finished the water. "Then who did?"

He set the glass aside and slid her shoulders down onto the pillow. "I have something for your sunburn." Carefully he unrolled the three napkins he'd soaked in water and witch hazel; one he laid directly over her face and with the other two he wrapped her forearms. "I'm afraid you're going to hurt some tomorrow. Your skin is pretty badly burned."

"It was worth it," she said on a sigh. "I said goodbye to Cissy."

Zane flinched. He still couldn't face seeing Celeste's grave. Maybe he never would.

"Nathan—"

"Zane," he corrected. "It's been Zane ever since I was ten years old and my baby sister couldn't say 'Nathaniel.'"

"Zane, then. If you didn't leave the roses, then who did?"

"Damned if I know," he muttered.

"You haven't visited her grave, have you?" Even muffled under the wet napkin, her voice sounded accusing.

"No, I have not."

"Why?"

He lifted the cloth from one of her slim forearms and swung it in the air, then settled it again. "I don't know why. Well, yes, I do know."

He swung the other napkin to cool it. "I— As long as I don't see her grave, she's not really gone."

Winifred pulled the cloth from her face and stared up at him. "But you saw her buried!"

Zane took the napkin from her hand and turned away to flap it in the air. "Yes, I know that I was there, or at least my body was there. Much of it I don't remember."

"Oh," she breathed. "I felt that way when our mother died. Cissy was probably too young to remember much, but for years afterward it was as if I had dreamed it, the funeral, and Papa weeping. There are still parts I don't recall clearly."

Zane folded the cooled cloth and laid it across her forehead. Her hair was loose, he noted, spread out on the pillow in a tumble of dark waves. It smelled faintly of cloves. Carnations, he guessed. Celeste's hair had smelled like some kind of mousse.

"Nath—Zane—you must visit Cissy's grave. I think it would help."

He choked back a harsh laugh. *Help? Nothing would help.* Nothing would ever be the same again.

"No," he said at last.

She held his gaze, the blue-green eyes he knew so well unblinking. Celeste had never challenged him like this. He found he didn't like it.

"No," he said again. "You have more guts than I do, Winifred. And while I take exception to your bluntness, I envy you your courage."

By the time Winifred had thought up a proper retort, she heard the door to her bedroom close behind him.

\* \* \*

In the morning, Winifred found the skin of her face and arms stiff and so parched her cheeks and arms stung. And her nose... She could not bear to look at it in the mirror over the yellow-painted chest in the bedroom. Gingerly she drew on a soft paisley skirt and shirtwaist, braided her hair and descended the stairs. She'd overslept. And, oh, how she needed a cup of Sam's coffee!

But Sam was not in the kitchen. And the saucepan she'd used to heat the baby's bottle still sat on the stove.

The back door swung open and Zane tramped in, a load of firewood stacked along one arm. "Morning," he said. "Sam's not going to be with us for a few more hours."

"It isn't chicken pox, is it?"

"Hardly. Too much hard cider at Uncle Charlie's last night." He dumped the wood into the wood box and bent to stir up the coals in the stove. "I'll make the coffee this morning."

The doorbell clanged.

"Damn that thing." Zane clunked a hefty piece of oak into the firebox and went to answer it.

Voices drifted from the entrance hall, a man's deep baritone and a child's trilling chatter. Winifred laid out plates and silverware on the dining table and tried not to listen.

"How'd she get up into the tree, Colonel?" Zane's voice.

"How does she get anywhere, Doc? She climbs or crawls. Some days I think she can fly."

She heard Zane's chuckle, then, "All right, Miss Manette, let's have a look at your arm."

"It hurts," the child said.

"I bet it does. Nevertheless, let me feel along the bone and see if you can make a fist. Ah, good. What were you doing up in the apple tree, hmm?"

"Looking for worms."

"Worms? Anyone ever tell you there's plenty of worms in the ground?"

"Not the right kind of worms," the girl insisted.

"Colonel, did she hit her head when she fell?"

"Don't know. Knocked the wind out of her, though," the man said.

"Might have a concussion," Zane said quietly. "Manette, does your head hurt?"

Silence. Apparently she was shaking her head.

"Now I want you to watch my finger."

More silence. Winifred set two cups down on the china saucers, taking care not to make any noise.

"Now, you look right into my eyes, all right?" Zane again.

"Your eyes are all shiny, Dr. Dee. And they're gray, just like Maman's."

"So they are. My mama's eyes were gray, too.

Give me your wrist, now. That's it. No, don't jerk it away. I want to feel your pulse."

"What's a pulse?"

"A pulse is your heart beating. It goes tha-lump, tha-lump. Here, you can feel mine."

"Yours is real loud!" Manette exclaimed.

"And yours is as normal as apple pie," Zane said.

Winifred had to smile. Zane was wonderful with the child.

"She's just fine, Colonel," Zane said. "Try to keep her out of the orchard from now on."

"Thanks, Zane. Jeanne will be in town tomorrow with a blackberry pie for you."

"She doesn't need to," Zane protested.

The man laughed. "Jeanne will never believe that."

The front door shut and Zane reappeared in the kitchen. "Spirited little tyke," he said with a smile. "Likes bugs and worms and everything else that crawls. Drives her father wild."

"And her mother?"

"Jeanne's used to it. Mothers get that way after a while. I know mine did."

"Did you like bugs?"

"No. I liked horses and swimming. And books." He grabbed the coffeepot. "I'll make some coffee."

"What about your baby sister? Did she like bugs?"

Zane looked purposefully at the handle of the coffeepot, then stared past her shoulder out the kitchen window. "Maggie died when she was five. Scarlet fever. That's when I decided to become a doctor."

Winifred could have bitten off her tongue. To lighten the pall that had fallen, she opened her mouth and blurted the first thing that came to mind. "I will scramble you some eggs this morning."

His dark eyebrows rose. "You can cook?"

"Well, not much. Growing up, we always had a cook. But I wager that eggs are easy to scramble."

"Celeste couldn't cook a damn thing," he said quietly. And then he smiled.

It was the first real smile she'd ever seen on his face. For some reason it made her so happy she wanted to do something extra nice. Sam seemed to scramble eggs with no apparent effort; they must be easy to fix. She decided to make lots of them.

While Zane made coffee, Winifred found an iron frying pan and four eggs. She shooed Zane out of the kitchen and set to work. She heated the pan over the hottest part of the stove, cracked all four eggs into it at once and smashed them together with a fork.

They congealed instantly into rubbery globs

that looked nothing like the creamy golden eggs Sam had set before her.

Apprehensively she scooped the mess out onto Zane's plate and set it before him. He sat looking at it for a long minute, gulped a swallow of coffee and looked up into her eyes.

"You can't cook a damn thing, either, can you?" he said softly.

And then he smiled again.

# Chapter Four

Zane didn't want to hurt Winifred's feelings about the plate of hard, dry scrambled eggs she'd served him. But when Sam staggered into the kitchen full of apologies for sleeping late, Zane left him in charge of Rosemarie and walked down to make hospital rounds, check on Sarah Rose's grandson and his chicken pox, then ended up, as he'd planned, at the Smoke River Hotel dining room.

"Scrambled eggs, please, Rita."

"Sure, Doc. Just come from the hospital, didja? How's the sheriff's new twins?"

"Maddie and the babies are doing well. Can't say the same for the sheriff, though. Seems he's been at the hospital the last twenty-four hours. Can't seem to take his eyes off his twin sons."

A wide grin split the waitress's round face. "Don't blame him, Doc. Our Johnny's never been a father before. New babies take some gettin' used to."

A plate of perfectly scrambled eggs appeared within minutes, and after he doused them liberally with catsup, he dug in. Rita hung at his elbow with the coffeepot.

"Guess you heard Johnny's been studyin' those law books Miss Maddie gave him. Gonna run for judge next election."

"When will that be?" Zane bit a half circle into his toast. Jericho Silver—Johnny, as Rita called him—was a good man. Honest. Intelligent. Hardworking. He'd make an excellent judge.

"If he gets elected he can stay home nights, feeding those twins."

Rita grinned. "Oh, he'll get elected all right, Doc. I'm his campaign manager."

Zane saluted her with his empty cup. Just as Rita lifted the pot to fill it, Zane froze. Good God, Winifred was entering the restaurant. The moment she spied him she frowned, wiped it off her face, then let it return and crossed the room to his table.

"Are those scrambled eggs?" she demanded.

He rose and invited her to sit down. "Rita, bring another plate, will you?"

"And some scrambled eggs, please," Winifred added.

They stared across the table at each other for a long minute.

"Quite a coincidence, isn't it?" he said at last. "Meeting here like this."

"Maybe not so much. We're probably both hungry after my disastrous attempt in the kitchen this morning."

"Yes," he said. "We are. Both hungry, I mean." He wondered at himself the instant the suggestive word crossed his lips. Thank God she didn't seem to hear.

Rita plopped a plate down in front of Winifred, and with an apologetic look at him, she lifted her fork. "This afternoon Sam is going to teach me how to scramble eggs."

Zane stared at her. Celeste had never exchanged more than two sentences with Sam, and she'd certainly never asked him to teach her anything about cooking.

"But before my egg lesson," Winifred continued, "there is something I'd like to discuss with you."

Zane's nerves went on alert. "Now?"

"No, not now. Later."

"I'll be at the hospital later."

Very deliberately she laid her fork on the plate. "The truth is you don't want to talk to me, do you? I can understand your not liking me, but—"

"I do like you." Oh, God, had he really said that? He drew in a long breath. "I apologize. That came out wrong. What I mean is we have nothing to discuss."

"It's about Celeste."

"Especially if it's about Celeste. She wanted the piano and all her music books shipped back to you at the conservatory, and her clothes—"

"Her clothes are too small for me, Zane. And she loved the color pink. I detest pink."

"I detest pink, too, but…" His voice thickened. "But I loved it on Celeste."

Winifred nodded. "I don't need the piano," she said quietly. "It brings back painful memories."

"Oh? What the hell do you think it does to *me*?" Instantly he regretted snapping at her. He waited, watching her coffee cup jiggle when she picked it up. Her fingers were trembling.

"Sorry. Guess I'm strung up a little tight these days."

"Well, so am I."

They stared at each other across the table for a long minute, and then Winifred dropped her eyes.

"Zane, when Cissy met you, she and I were about to go on tour. London, Paris, Vienna. Even Rome, which Cissy didn't want to visit because she feared it would be too hot. Did you know about this?"

"No, I did not know. She never told me. All I know is that there was a piano recital one night at the medical college and Celeste was playing. She wore some kind of flowing pink gown, chiffon, I guess it's called. And she was the most beautiful creature I'd ever seen. I fell in love with her during her first piece. Chopin, I remember. An étude."

"In A-flat," Winifred supplied.

"Is that what you want to discuss—the music tour you and Celeste were planning?"

"No, it isn't. It's, well, something else."

Their eyes met and held. Hers were distant. Troubled. He didn't know what his eyes betrayed, but all at once she blinked and bit her lip.

"Zane, I am trying to understand about Celeste. She was so smitten she left everything we had planned to run away with you. I…" She swallowed. "I am trying hard to forgive her for leaving it all behind. And for dying," she added, her voice pinched.

"I am trying, as well," he said quietly. "Part of me is hurt and angry that she—that she is gone." Another part of him, the part he could scarcely acknowledge to himself, much less share with Winifred Von Dannen, was his weariness. He was tired of the constant grinding pain. And he was hungry. Yes, that was the word, hungry for something else.

The trouble was, he didn't have the slightest idea what that might be.

Winifred sipped her coffee and looked at him over the rim of the cup. "It must be very hard," she said at last.

For a moment he couldn't speak over the ache in his throat. "It is hard," he said at last. "You have no idea how hard."

She looked at him with tears pooling in her eyes and all at once he could take no more. "I'll be at the hospital."

Without another word he shoved back his chair and strode out the door onto the street.

Winifred watched him through the front dining room window, his long-legged gait decisive, angry, his shoulders hunched forward as if warding off a chill wind. *What wouldn't she give to have met him before Cissy had.*

Her coffee cup clanked onto the saucer. Where on earth had *that* thought come from?

"Somethin' wrong with your breakfast, ma'am?" Rita stood frowning at her elbow. "Never seen Doc bolt outta here like that."

"Oh, no, Rita. The eggs were very good, just right in fact. Dr. Dougherty said he had to go to the hospital."

"Huh," the woman said. "That man's working too hard, if ya ask me. Never takes a day off, up all hours of the day and night. Ever since his wife died it's like he never stops runnin'."

Winifred tried to smile, but her mouth wouldn't work right. She clenched her lower lip between her teeth to stop its trembling. She was a silly, sentimental fool.

"I'll jest put the meal on his account. Yours, too."

Outside on the boardwalk she stood surveying the streets of the small town she found herself in, then on impulse started down a pretty maple-lined lane. Five houses from the corner an attractive yellow two-story house caught her eye. The white picket fence surrounding the property was thick with yellow roses, the same roses she'd found on Cissy's grave yesterday.

Just as she drew abreast of the gate, the front door opened and a handsome gray-haired gentleman descended the steps. Clutched in his hand was a bouquet of the same yellow roses.

"Mornin'," he said as he unlatched the gate. "Another fine day we're havin'."

Winifred stared at the man. "What? Oh, yes. Excuse me, but…forgive my asking, but what will you do with those roses?"

He dropped his gaze to the bouquet. "These? Why, I'm takin' these to the graveyard where Miss Celeste—" He broke off and peered at her with startling blue eyes.

"Say, you must be her sister from the East."

"Why, yes, I am. How did you guess that?"

"Weren't hard, seein' as how you look a lot like her. Name's Rooney Cloudman, ma'am. I was an admirer of yer sister."

She held out her hand. "Winifred Von Dannen."

Mr. Cloudman shifted the roses to his left hand and grasped hers in a finger-crunching grip. "Miss Celeste, she liked roses, so I take some to her grave every day. Sure do miss her piano-playin'. Used to sneak up on Doc's porch and set in the swing jest listenin'. Most beautiful music I ever heard."

Winifred swallowed hard, unable to speak for a long moment. "Yes, she was quite gifted."

"I never let on 'bout me listenin'. Figured Doc wouldn't mind, but I was afeared she'd stop playin' if she knew."

"I am sure she would have been pleased, Mr. Cloudman."

He gave her a wide smile. "Whyn't you go on into the house and introduce yerself to Sarah Rose. She loved Miss Celeste's music, too. Me, I'm off to the cemetery." He tipped his battered wide-brimmed hat and ambled on down the street.

Winifred didn't feel like talking to anyone, especially about Cissy, so she decided to return to the doctor's house on the hill and take her cooking lesson from Sam. She snapped off a single yellow rose from the stems rambling along the fence, spun in place and marched back to the big hill and Dr. Dougherty's beautiful white house.

In the hospital foyer, Zane was stopped by Samuel Graham, the physician whose name the hospital bore. The older man laid a gentle hand on Zane's shoulder.

"How are you managing, son?"

"Well enough, I suppose."

"Sorry I couldn't be here when Sarah's grandson took sick. I was called away to Gillette Springs for an emergency appendectomy."

"Don't give it a thought, Samuel. You know Sarah always brings one of her apple pies—that's a large payment for a small favor." He tried to accompany the statement with a smile but somehow this morning he couldn't manage it.

The hand on his shoulder tightened. "Don't mind my sayin' so, Zane, but you look fatigued. And your eyes…you been drinking?"

"Some," Zane admitted. More than "some" on the days Celeste's death cut particularly deep. His medical partner had sharp eyes.

"Celeste's sister is here from St. Louis."

Doc Graham's salt-and-pepper eyebrows rose. "That so? Must be why you're frowning. Is she a trial?"

Zane sighed. "She is not." Winifred was far from a trial, as Samuel put it. She was…he didn't know what she was, just that he liked having her around.

"She's older than Celeste. More…mature."

The keen-eyed physician nodded. "I did rounds at eight this morning. Just leaving now to go back to the boardinghouse. Sarah serves lunch early on Sunday."

Zane blinked. It was Sunday? Good God, he was losing track of the days again. "Anything new?"

"Mrs. Madsen's leg ulcer looks better. I'd keep her in bed an extra day, give her some rest from that husband of hers. You'd think he had the only milk cows in the county the way he coddles them."

"But not his wife," Zane observed. "That how she fell, a cow knocked her down?"

Doc Graham nodded. "You might look in on Whitey Poletti. Keeps insisting he's well and itching to get back to his barbershop. Testy, too, so watch yourself."

Zane had had a bellyful of Whitey. With each haircut the man insisted Zane also needed a shave. He'd tried it once; Whitey had sent him home with some girly-smelling cologne that brought on Celeste's asthma.

"And Zane," the older man said. "Cut Nurse

Sorensen some slack today, will you? It's her birthday."

Graham pivoted toward the hospital entrance and Zane watched his head disappear as he went down the front steps.

He checked on Mrs. Madsen's leg ulcer, Whitey Poletti's gall bladder incision and finally Sheriff Silver's wife and the twins he'd delivered twenty-four hours ago.

"Good morning, Maddie. You ready to go home tomorrow?"

The sheriff's wife grinned up at him from her hospital bed. "*I* am ready, Dr. Dougherty. I'm not sure about Jericho."

"All new fathers feel somewhat overwhelmed. I know I did. I couldn't quite believe such a tiny human being was my responsibility. And ever since Celeste—" He stopped short.

Maddie Silver gazed up at him with concerned eyes. "I am so sorry about your wife, Doc. I know I've said that before, but, well, you've been on my mind ever since the funeral."

Zane took her small, capable hand in his. "And you've been on my mind, as well. It isn't every day a doctor gets to deliver twins. Especially for a Pinkerton agent."

He checked Maddie over, asked whether the twins were nursing regularly and left to seek out

Elvira Sorensen. Elvira was the full-time nurse the hospital employed; Zinnia Langenfelder worked part-time as a nurse's aide.

"Elvira, I want you to take the rest of the day and evening off."

"What? But why? You know I always work the Sunday shift."

"Zinnia can cover for you. You go on over to Uncle Charlie's bakery for one of those lemon cakes you're so fond of. Tell him to put it on my account."

He planted a kiss on the older woman's cheek. "Happy birthday, Elvira." Then he strode out of the hospital and down the front steps.

"Well," Elvira huffed, patting her hot cheeks. "I never did understand that man. But he's a good 'un, I'd say."

## Chapter Five

The doorbell rang on and off all afternoon. By the time Zane returned from the hospital, patients lined the entry hall. First, Noralee Ness tearfully presented two itchy, splotchy forearms and an inflamed forehead. "I was scared to show Mama cuz I thought I had leprosy," she wailed.

"Why, it's nothing but poison oak," Zane assured her. He sent her off to her father's mercantile with a prescription for calamine lotion.

Next, burly Ike Bruhn unwrapped a torn and bloody thumb he'd smashed while building a chicken coop. Zane cleaned and bandaged the wound, dosed him with two aspirin and a shot of brandy for the pain and sent him off with strict instructions for keeping his thumb clean and dry.

His last patient was Sarah Rose, and he was surprised at her presence. "Oh, it's not about my grandson, Mark," the rosy-cheeked woman assured him. "It's about me. Lately my heart's been actin' funny, kinda skittery, and I want to know if…if…well, maybe I shouldn't be thinking about so much activity at my age."

Zane had her undo the top buttons of her dress and laid his stethoscope against her chemise. "What do you mean, 'so much activity'? You doing anything unusually strenuous lately?"

"Well, no. I mean not yet."

Sarah's heartbeat sounded strong and regular. "Not yet?"

The older woman's cheeks grew even more rosy.

"Sarah, why come to me when Doc Graham lives at your boardinghouse?"

"That's just it, you see. I didn't want Doc to know I was worried. It's kinda private."

"Private? Just what is worrying you, Sarah?"

Sarah wet her lips. "Do you think my heart is strong enough to, well, engage in some, well, spooning?"

Zane sat back. "Spooning? You mean making love?"

"Doc, hush! Someone might hear."

Zane lowered his voice. "What, exactly, are you contemplating?"

Sarah leaned forward. "Marriage," she whispered. "I'm thinking about getting married."

He must have misheard the woman. Marriage? At her age? She must be over sixty! And who—?

"Rooney's asked me to marry him, Doc. I want to, but I wouldn't dare accept him and then die of heart failure on our honeymoon. It'd make him mighty unhappy."

Zane tried like hell to keep a straight face. "Sarah, you're in no danger of dying anytime soon no matter what you do, honeymoon or otherwise."

She clasped his hand in both of hers. "Oh, thank you! I was so worried, you see. Thank you." She rebuttoned her dress and stood up. "I brought an apple pie for you cuz you came to see Mark yesterday. I left it in the kitchen with Sam."

"Sarah, I do love your apple pies, but you don't owe me anything." He squeezed her shoulder and walked her to the door of his office. When he heard the front door close he sank down behind his wide oak desk and poured himself a brandy.

So Sarah Rose wanted to marry again. Well, why not? She'd been widowed almost thirty years; she deserved some joy in life. A lot of joy, in fact. He had a particular soft spot for a woman who could run a boardinghouse year in, year out without becoming soured on humanity. He also had a soft spot for anyone willing to risk their heart in marriage. He'd sure as hell never do it again.

Losing Celeste had left his life so bleak that

sometimes he didn't want to go on. But he knew he had to, for Rosemarie.

He lifted his glass to Sarah Rose, downed the contents in one gulp and poured another. This one he nursed while idly leafing through the stack of medical journals on the corner of his desk. Nothing startling and nothing new. Sometimes he thought medicine back East would benefit from a dose of Out West Indian remedies.

He continued to sip and read until he heard the front door open and saw Winifred glide past his window. After a moment he heard the rhythmic creak-creak of the porch swing. She had wanted to speak with him about something, he remembered. Now would be as good a time as any. He gulped the last of the brandy and pushed away from the desk.

A breeze had come up, scented with pine and the honeysuckle that drooped from the porch posts. Celeste had loved the smell of honeysuckle, even though in the summer it made her sneeze. He sucked in a breath at the bolt of anguish that laced across his chest.

Winifred sat rocking in the swing with a sleeping Rosemarie cradled in her arms. She looked up when he closed the front door.

"May I join you?"

"Of course. It's your porch, and your swing."

Zane frowned. That sounded unusually crisp

for Winifred. Or perhaps he just did not know her well. He settled an arm's length away and they rocked in silence for a while. He hoped she couldn't smell the brandy on his breath.

"At breakfast you said you wanted to talk to me about something?" He didn't really want to talk, but whatever she had on her mind it was better to get it over with.

"Yes, I did. I wanted to... I want..."

Ah. She didn't really want to talk, either. "We don't have to talk, Winifred. We could just watch the sun go down behind the hills." He didn't like it when a woman "wanted to talk."

"We do have to talk." Her voice was oddly flat and a ripple of unease snaked up his spine.

"About?" he prompted.

She bent her head over his daughter, then raised it and looked straight into his eyes. "About Rose-marie. I—I want to take her back to St. Louis with me. I want to raise her."

He stopped the swing so abruptly her neck jerked back.

"Are you crazy? What on earth makes you—?"

"Think this is a good idea?" she finished for him.

"For starters, yes." Zane kept his tone civil, but inside he seethed. Suddenly he wished he had another shot of brandy in his hand.

"It is a good idea, Zane. I think Cissy might have wanted it."

"You know nothing about what Celeste wanted." His voice was low and angry, and he didn't care.

"A child," she continued. "Especially a girl, should have a mother. Cissy and I grew up without a mother, and it was like…like always feeling hungry for something."

Zane wrapped one hand around the chain supporting the swing and clenched the other into a fist. "I am Rosemarie's father, Winifred. She is *mine. My* daughter. *My* responsibility."

"But I could give her advantages, living in the East. Good schools. Music lessons. You cannot offer such things out here so far from civilization."

He counted to twenty to keep his temper from making him say something he'd regret. "What gives you the right to disparage the life I can offer my child? We have a school. I can hire music teachers or art lessons or anything else my daughter needs." His voice shook with fury and something else. Fear. He could not face losing Rosemarie, too.

"But—"

He waited until she looked directly at him. "Dammit, Winifred, you waltz out here and expect me to give up my daughter to a citified stranger with expensive clothes and high-faluting conservatory training? What do you take me for?"

That hit home. He could see the hurt in her eyes, but he was too angry to soften his words.

"The answer is no," he shot. "It will always be no. Rosemarie is all I have of Celeste, and I will never—"

"Zane, please listen to me."

"Winifred, for God's sake, I love my daughter more than anything on this earth. Nothing, *nothing* you or anyone else could offer her can make any difference."

Tears now sheened her cheeks, and while he felt a small hiccup of regret inside his chest, he couldn't respond. Very slowly she placed Rosemarie in his lap and, keeping her face averted, slipped out of the swing and stepped quickly into the house.

Zane finished two more brandies before Sam called him to supper. Winifred did not appear, and he sent the houseboy upstairs to check on her.

"Lady say she not hungry, Boss."

"Take her a chicken sandwich and some tea," he ordered.

Sam folded his hands at his waist. "She not eat it."

"Take it up anyway, dammit!"

He found he wasn't hungry, either. His head began to pound with the familiar ache he'd felt ever since Celeste died, and after sitting and staring for an hour at the plate of food before him he stalked into the kitchen, grabbed the warmed baby bottle out of Sam's hand and plodded up the stairs to feed his daughter.

The next morning when Winifred entered the dining room, Sam poured her coffee and shook his head. "Eyes look red, missy."

Winifred brushed her fingers over her swollen eyelids. She had wept most of the night and slept little. "It's—it's my hay fever, I expect." She lifted the cup to her lips.

Sam bent at the waist and tipped his head to peer into her face. "Maybe so," he pronounced. "Boss eyes look funny, too."

The houseboy's keen black eyes glinted.

Winifred took a swallow of coffee. "You don't miss much, do you, Sam?"

"Miss not much," he agreed with a grin. "Boss never fool me."

Nor, Winifred reflected, had she. She huffed out a sigh. Knowing that Zane was distressed did not ease her own anguish. She'd done more than make a mess of her offer to raise Rosemarie; she'd alienated the doctor, perhaps even made him resent her. Lord's sake, would he prevent her from visiting her niece in the future? She couldn't bear that.

She clamped her mouth shut and pushed away the plate of eggs and toast Sam laid before her. She couldn't eat. If she opened her mouth she knew a sob would erupt.

"Must eat, missy. Good fight need full belly."

She blinked at Sam in surprise. A good fight?

He planted his slippered feet at her side and propped his hands on his hips. "You eat," he ordered. "Then I teach how to make biscuit."

"Biscuits!"

Sam nodded. "Next lesson after tumbled eggs."

Oh, for heaven's sake. All right, she'd eat something.

Sam was as stubborn as Zane.

"Doctor leave early," the houseboy volunteered. "Go on horse to make home calls. You watch baby, I do washing of diapers."

After breakfast, Winifred settled in the library to read, keeping her eye on Rosemarie where she slept beside her in a pink flannel-lined laundry basket. When the baby woke, she sat on the floor beside her and let her play with her forefinger. "Oh, you darling, perfect child, do you know how exquisite you are? You have eyes just like my sister's, yes, you do."

She picked the baby up and buried her nose against the child's soft neck. "And you smell so sweet, like…like a little rose."

She rocked the soft bundle in her arms until a faint cry signaled the baby was hungry. Before she could stir, Sam laid a warm bottle of milk in her free hand and padded quietly away.

By evening, after she had changed and fed Rosemarie again, Zane still had not returned. After a supper of thick potato soup and hunks of fresh-baked bread, Winifred moved the wheeled bassinet from Zane's room into her own. If the baby woke during the night, Winifred could tend to her. She hoped he wouldn't mind.

She lay awake reading the volume of Words-worth poems by candlelight until long past moon-rise, then puffed out the light and closed her still-swollen eyes.

For the next two days she did not catch even a glimpse of the doctor. She knew he came in from the hospital late at night because Sam reported on his activities. And he left the house before she was awake.

To pass the time each afternoon she talked to Rosemarie and let her play with her fingers, fed her and rocked her for hours with a fullness in her throat. Whenever she lifted the baby into her arms, an absurd bolt of joy bloomed inside her chest, and when Rosemarie opened her extraor-dinary eyes and looked at her one evening Win-ifred knew she had fallen head over heels in love with her niece.

When the baby was fussy Winifred found herself humming half-remembered lullabies, and when she couldn't remember the words, she simply made them up. Mornings, while Rosemarie slept, she spent time in the kitchen with Sam. In two days she mastered not only biscuits but pancakes and bread and even piecrust. Piecrust! Just imagine. She might be the only concert pianist in the country who could roll out a piecrust! She couldn't wait for the next basket of blueberries or blackberries a patient brought for the doctor; she would bake the most delicious pie he ever ate.

Every morning the entry hall filled up with waiting patients, and every afternoon Sam stepped in to send them all down to the hospital because the doctor had left. After two days without a glimpse of Zane, Winifred knew with certainty that he was avoiding her.

At breakfast the following morning, Sam clucked over her like a mother hen. "Doctor visit lady wife's grave yesterday."

"Oh?"

"Then come home drink brandy all night."

The houseboy closed his lips with finality and sloshed hot coffee into her cup. "Boss sleep late today. Go to hospital in afternoon, then see patients here today."

One of them, young Noralee Ness, brought a quart jar of fresh-picked blackberries. All afternoon Winifred labored in the kitchen over her piecrust, while Sam offered cryptic comments every now and then. "Not more rolling, missy. Make crust like shoe leather."

The pie emerged from the oven golden and bubbling purple juice from between the lattice strips. Winifred inhaled the fruity scent and smiled. It would be a peace offering for Zane.

By suppertime, Zane still had not returned from the hospital. Winifred ate a quiet, solitary supper with Rosemarie sleeping in her basket on the chair next to her. Disappointment gnawed at her.

She fed and rocked the baby, cut a huge slab of her pie and left it on a plate in the doctor's office, along with a fork and a napkin. Then she dragged herself up to bed with legs that felt like wooden fence posts. She had made an enemy of Cissy's husband and Rosemarie's father. She crawled into bed and pulled the bassinet close.

She closed her eyes but couldn't sleep. Was Zane so put out with her he wouldn't let her visit again?

In the morning, the bassinet was gone. Winifred sat bolt upright in bed and stared at her closed bedroom door. Zane must have come in while she slept and rolled the bassinet back to his bedroom. At least that meant he was home. She prayed he wasn't angry with her for moving the baby to her room. And for once she could do what she'd waited days to accomplish, make an apology.

She dressed in a light blue dimity wrapper, hurriedly braided her hair and pinned the coils at her nape and sped down the stairs to breakfast.

Zane rose as she entered the dining room. A telltale smear of purple juice on his lower lip hinted that he'd sampled her pie this morning. Something inside her began to sing.

"Good morning."

"Good morning. One of your patients brought some blackberries yesterday, so I—"

His dark eyebrows rose. "Are you saying *you* made the pie?"

"Yes, I… Sam showed me how and—"

His sudden smile startled her into silence. "I'm surprised," he said. "And impressed."

Winifred knew she was blushing. The distinctly odd expression in Zane's gray eyes confirmed it. Instantly she found it hard to breathe. He looked and looked at her without speaking until the flesh on her bare forearms formed tiny goose bumps.

"Winifred?"

"Y-yes?"

Zane watched her eyes widen. They were like Celeste's, yes, but a shade darker. And at this moment they looked…apprehensive.

"I owe you an apology."

The morning air was already stifling, and the sun had scarcely cleared the mountains to the east. Perhaps that was why her cheeks were so pink. He loosened his shirt collar in the oppressive heat.

She looked down at the tablecloth, at the door leading to the kitchen, everywhere but at him. He held his breath until she spoke.

"I rather thought I owed *you* the apology. I had no right to…" She swallowed and looked up at him, her eyes shiny. "Perhaps a child's place really is with her father."

"Perhaps," he suggested quickly, "we should forgive each other and have breakfast."

A beaming Sam slipped into the room, a platter of eggs and bacon in one hand, the coffeepot in the other. "Have biscuits, too," he announced. "And jar of apricot jam from Missy Madsen. For ulcer, she say."

"Ah, yes." Zane nodded. "Sent her home yesterday to rest. Apparently she made jam instead. Sometimes I wonder what good a physician's advice is."

Winifred continued to study him.

He saw that she was struggling to articulate the question in her eyes. "What is it, Winifred? What do you want to ask?"

She blinked and licked her lips. "How do you know I want to ask anything?"

"I am a doctor. I was trained to read people's eyes and facial expressions. Often they reveal more than heart rates or blood pressure, or even fevers."

He wished she wouldn't run her tongue over her lips that way; something inside him flickered to life when she did it. Something he didn't want to think about.

God in heaven, every fiber of his being ached to hear Celeste's voice, feel her warmth beside him at night. His brain could acknowledge that she was gone, but part of him still could not accept it. Maybe he never would.

The lazy morning heat pressed down on him. He didn't want to move; he just wanted to escape to someplace cool and green where he didn't have to think.

An idea popped into his brain. He discounted it immediately, then shook his head. Yes, why not?

# Chapter Six

"Winifred, would you care to go swimming this afternoon?"

She frowned. He could see her hesitation, but the more he thought about it the more he thought it was a good idea. He knew she didn't like him and he'd hurt her feelings. He wanted to make it up to her in some way. He pressed on. "It's beastly hot, and I have no duties at the hospital until evening. I often go to a place, we call it a 'swimming hole' out here, where the river widens into a pool, like a lagoon. I go there often in the summer, usually on horseback."

"I'm afraid I have nothing proper to wear for riding. Or for swimming, either."

"Sam can find you something. Besides, no one else ever goes to this spot, so no one will see you."

"No one but you." She sounded half tempted and half disapproving.

"I won't look, I promise."

"I do not believe you, Zane. But it is too tempting to escape this awful heat, so yes, let's do go swimming."

Zane held back a smile. Celeste's older sister was more adventurous than Celeste had been. More open to trying new things, like baking a pie. And more tolerant of human error.

Or was she? He watched her stuff the last of her toast in her mouth and gulp down her coffee. He knew nothing about her, really. Every day she surprised him.

She rose from the table and started for the kitchen. "Sam? Could you find a riding skirt for me in Celeste's closet? And maybe..."

Her voice faded. Zane sat in the humming silence for a full minute. Celeste's riding clothes would never fit her older sister. Winifred's build was not delicate like his wife's.

Winifred was more shapely. More fluid when she moved. More...handsome, that was the word. And Lord help him, she was much more uninhibited in both her speech and her actions.

He got to his feet and headed for the stable. He'd take the buggy instead. It was too hot for horseback riding.

Winifred was silent for most of the drive out to the swimming hole, and finally it got under Zane's skin. What was she thinking about? Was she still angry about the abominable way he'd spoken to her three days ago? He tried to keep his mind on guiding the gray mare hitched to the buggy, but the woman who sat next to him on the leather seat kept capturing his attention.

She was interested in everything, the larches and sugar maples starting to turn scarlet and gold with the onset of fall, the red-tailed hawks that soared above, the deer they startled in the copse of birches as they approached the river, even the hazy purple mountains in the distance. Finally, she started to talk.

"What are those little yellow-and-brown birds in that tree?"

"Chickadees."

"And that big blue one with the long tail?"

"That's a blue jay. Steller's jay, it's called."

She laughed. "I should have guessed by the color." They rode in silence for another mile, and then she pointed at something on the ground. "What is that tangle of green fronds over by the riverbank?"

Zane had to laugh. "Mint. You've never seen mint growing in the wild? When we leave I'll cut some to take to Sam. He dries the leaves and brews outstanding mint tea."

"And that—" She broke off and sent him a

sidelong glance. "I'm asking too many questions, aren't I?"

He chuckled. "Not nearly enough." He had to admit he liked showing things to her, explaining things. Celeste had shown little interest in the countryside.

"How do you know all these things? Did you grow up in the West?"

"I grew up in a small town in New York. Albany."

"I grew up in a city. St. Louis."

"I'll wager you've never gone swimming in a river, have you?"

There was another long silence. "I've never gone swimming at all," she confessed. "Is this swimming hole very, um, deep?"

Zane shot her a look. Winifred couldn't swim? Why had she agreed to come?

The lane narrowed to mere wheel tracks, then curved around behind a stand of ash trees and emerged fifty yards from the lazily flowing river. He pulled the horse to a stop and climbed down.

"Over there." He waved one arm. "We walk from here."

Winifred clambered out, clutching a rolled-up bit of clothing. Celeste's bathing costume, he guessed. He'd never seen her wear it.

The lagoon-like pond where he liked to swim lay tucked in a bend in the river, screened by drooping willow and cottonwood trees. The water looked cool and inviting. Without thinking, he stripped off his muslin shirt, then stopped short.

She stared at him as if she'd never seen a man's bare chest before. Good God, perhaps she hadn't. Once again her cheeks turned rose-red. It never occurred to him that she might be…modest.

"Winifred, I—"

"Do you swim, um, naked?"

"Usually, yes. Today I'll keep my underdrawers on if you'd feel more comfortable."

She didn't answer for a long moment. "I will, uh, change into Cissy's bathing costume behind that shrub." She stepped over to a large huckleberry bush.

Zane shucked his trousers, sprinted to the water and dove in. Out of courtesy to Winifred he stayed facing away from her until he heard a soft splash behind him. When he turned he caught his breath.

She stood poised at the river's edge, swishing the toes of one foot in the water, and good God almighty, she filled every inch of Celeste's bathing garment. He turned away and swam to the far end of the pool, then stroked to the opposite end.

Before he reached it, he heard a yelp and a loud splash. When he looked back she was chest-deep in the river.

"How does one swim?" she called.

"Just put your arms out and bend forward and then shove off from the bottom."

To his surprise she did exactly as he said. Her head disappeared underwater, broke the surface, then sank once more. Just as he started to stroke toward her, she reemerged, her arms flailing, water spewing out of her mouth.

But she didn't call for help. Instead, she thrashed forward, trying to keep her head above water.

"Kick your legs," he yelled.

Suddenly she was ploughing through the water, her arms making sloppy waving motions, her eyes scrunched tightly closed.

"Winifred," he shouted. "Open your eyes."

"Can't," she called. "I'll drown."

That made him laugh out loud. She'd come this far; he'd let her discover the rest for herself.

He stroked to the far end of the pool and back again, then methodically swam ten or twelve additional lengths. When he pulled himself onto the sandy bank he was breathing hard.

Winifred was clumsily propelling herself in a ragged circle, but she had opened her eyes. Zane lay back on the warm sand and laid his arm over his face. He didn't want to watch her come out of the river. She'd be wet, and the too-small swimming suit would hide nothing. He couldn't help smiling at the picture he imagined, but he wouldn't embarrass her by actually looking.

He'd seen hundreds, maybe thousands, of women's bodies; but this woman was different. For one thing, she was his wife's sister.

But God, how he wanted to see her!

After half an hour she splashed out of the water with a triumphant cry. "I did it! I can swim!"

Zane kept his eyes closed.

"Did you see me? I was really swimming, wasn't I?"

"You were really swimming, Winifred. Congratulations."

Droplets of cool water hit his chest and still he didn't open his eyes. "Better get out of that wet suit," he ordered.

He prayed she would do just that. The temptation to open his eyes was overpowering.

He managed another sixty seconds, then caught a fleeting glimpse of her as she ducked behind the huckleberry bush. He groaned, got to his feet and dove into the water again for twelve more laps. When he emerged, Winifred sat on the bank, the skirt of her blue dimity dress hiked up to her calves, her bare toes digging into the sand. She looked like a happy child.

A lump as big as an orange lodged in his throat.

He had never seen Celeste look that young and un-
guarded. Never.

He propelled himself out of the river and strode
past her to yank on his trousers and shirt. He was
still short of breath, but this time he knew it had
nothing to do with swimming laps.

On the drive back to town, Winifred chattered
on about teaching herself to swim, about the chickadees, about gathering the mint, about everything.
Zane held onto the traces so tight his knuckles
ached but said nothing. His breath came in short
gusts, his brain swirled with a thousand thoughts.
Outrageous thoughts.

His wife's sister. He was attracted to his sister-
in-law!

When they reached the house, he tossed the
reins to Sam and bolted for his office and the
brandy decanter.

After supper that night, Zane went outside to
rock in the porch swing in the soft evening air,
sweet with honeysuckle. Then, to his horror, Winifred joined him.

They said nothing for a long time, then she
drew in a steadying breath and lightly touched
his arm.

"I must leave, Zane."

"I thought as much."

"I have a concert in two weeks, and I must prepare."

"Yes."

"I've grown to love Rosemarie. I would like to come back at Christmastime. If I may."

"Yes, of course."

"I will go tomorrow, then. The train leaves at noon."

He said nothing for a long moment. "I'll drive you to the station in the buggy."

"Thank you."

"We will miss you. All of us—Rosemarie and Sam and...and me."

There was nothing more to say. He felt as if a candle were being extinguished. It made no sense.

He rose abruptly, stalked inside the house and tramped upstairs to hold his baby daughter in his arms.

Winifred waited until his footsteps faded, then slipped through the front door and into his office and searched until she found the brandy decanter.

At eleven o'clock the following searingly hot morning, Zane drove Winifred to catch the train. Neither spoke. At the station he helped her down and carried her valise into the station house while she purchased her ticket.

He watched her fold the ticket into her reticule

and felt his gut clench. He was torn about her leaving. He would miss seeing her across the table at breakfast, miss watching her rocking his baby daughter to sleep, watching her thrash across the swimming hole learning to swim.

Oh, hell, he'd just miss her.

Yes, he was still grieving for Celeste. Yes, he was lonely. He'd thought he was so numb with grief he was dead inside.

But he'd miss Winifred.

On the other hand, he couldn't be around her. Shouldn't be around her. He was glad she was leaving.

The train was late and every minute they waited was awkward. Zane walked the length of the platform, stopped where Winifred stood waiting, her valise beside her, then walked another length. When he returned to her side she did not look at him.

Finally he couldn't stand it any longer. "Winifred?"

She looked up at his voice. "Yes, Zane?"

"I'm glad you came. I dreaded it. Dreaded meeting you, at first, but…"

"But you're glad I am leaving." She gave him a wobbly smile.

"Yes. And no."

She held up her hand. "Don't explain. Please don't."

He nodded. He couldn't explain even if he wanted to.

Suddenly she pivoted away from him. "There's the train. I hear the whistle." She moved toward the tracks. He grabbed up her valise and followed.

The locomotive engine whooshed past, slowing to position the passenger car in front of the loading platform. Winifred kept her back to him until she reached the iron boarding step, then turned to face him. With one hand she reached for the valise he carried, and with the other she reached for him.

He enveloped her hand in both of his, opened his mouth to say goodbye and found he had no voice.

She smiled at him again. "You don't have to say anything, Zane."

He cleared his throat. "Come back," he said.

She pressed her lips together and inclined her head. Tears shone in her eyes.

September 20th

Dear Zane,

My concert on the seventeenth went well— actually better than I expected. I didn't have a speck of stage fright, as I usually do. Cissy never had qualms about performing; I was always the one with shaking hands and a fluttery heart. I played some of her favorites—

Brahms waltzes and a Beethoven sonata or two. No Chopin.

My teaching load at the conservatory will increase with the new term beginning in January. I have plenty of students already—more than the other professors—and one or two intermediates show considerable promise. Often I look at them and wonder if I was ever that young. They are so serious, so disciplined, so full of hope.

Next month I will play in Chicago with an orchestra, and after that in New York City and then Boston. My career in music—the life both Cissy and I dreamed of since we were in pinafores—is terribly important to me. Even more, now that Cissy is gone, and that is strange in a way because I could never have imagined doing this without her. But it is everything to me now, perhaps because... Oh, I don't know, really.

I am working very hard, harder than last term, with many more concert engagements. By November I will surely need a rest.

One of my fellow faculty members, Millicent Erhard, has invited me to her home in Rochester for two weeks; she promises lots of music "for fun." That will be a relief.

Kiss Rosemarie for me.

Winifred

October 3rd

Dear Winifred,

Rosemarie thrives, though half the county is down with influenza. I have been at the hospital day and night as our permanent nurse, Elvira Sorensen—did you meet her?—came down with it last week and I am training another woman who is not nearly as conscientious. Good nurses are hard to find.

You will not believe this next: Sam is getting married! He has been saving the salary I pay him, and adding his winnings at fan-tan, which he plays with Uncle Charlie—the baker, remember? Three months ago he sent to his family in China for a "respectable girl with not a loud voice." He included money for her fare to Portland, and she should arrive before Christmas. I am enlarging Sam's room off the kitchen and installing a small bathroom for them as well.

I would like to give him a wedding gift, but do not know what would be appropriate. Perhaps you will have some ideas.

One of my patients, a farmer by the name of Peter Jensen, is holding a winter dance in his barn on Saturday. He wants me to come in case a fight breaks out. Why not the sheriff, I wonder? But Sam is urging me to "get out of house." The weather will be crisp. I have given up brandy so must make do with hot cider.

I wonder what you will think of New York City, and Rochester. It should be snowing by then. I also wonder if you can ice-skate. It was my greatest pleasure in the winter when I was growing up, and it cost little so it was no strain on Mother's finances.
Zane

PS: Sam has adopted a stray kitten "for mice in the pantry," which I don't believe for one minute.

## Chapter Seven

A snowy November passed slowly, with nothing for Winifred to do but practice for her next concert and teach. She thought she would go mad cooped up inside until the trip to Rochester with Millicent. But the week away from her duties passed quickly, and now nothing could assuage her restlessness.

Her piano students performed flawlessly at the winter recital the conservatory held each year, and in mid-December the term ended. As soon as she could escape the endless faculty meetings to plan for next term, she purchased her train ticket and wired Zane.

Just think! Rosemarie might be crawling by now. She shopped for a frilly dress for her and tiny soft slippers to match, then on impulse bought a handsome quilted comforter for Sam and his new bride and had it shipped via Wells Fargo. It should arrive before she did. And, she hoped, before Sam's new bride from China made her appearance.

The night before the train departed for the West she found she couldn't sleep. Rosemarie would be almost five months old by now. She missed the baby's grip on her forefinger. She missed holding her in her arms and singing nonsense songs to her. Missed seeing her grow and change. She even missed Zane.

He wrote that he swam in the river right up until the first frost. It was a wonder *he* didn't catch influenza. Or perhaps he had, and that was why there had been no answer to her telegram.

At four in the morning she could lie still no longer. She climbed out of her narrow bed and began to pack her valise.

The train from the East was late, held up in Colorado by an avalanche across the tracks, Charlie, the stationmaster, explained. Zane hoped Winifred had a warm winter coat and gloves or a muff to protect her hands. He paced back and forth on the platform, then went inside for hot coffee and the latest news, then began pacing again.

He guessed he was nervous. He hadn't been this nervous when Winifred had first arrived in Smoke River last August, but he hadn't known her then. He shouldn't be nervous now, but there it was; his heartbeat wouldn't calm down and his palms were damp.

When at last the arriving locomotive sounded a warning whistle, Zane stepped forward. The train chuffed to a stop amid a cloud of white steam and sat huffing on the track while the passengers debarked. He held his breath until he saw her, swathed in a long black coat and wearing a black fur hat. She looked so beautiful his chest ached.

"Winifred!"

She spotted him and waved one hand. They fought their way toward each other through a throng of people, and by the time they were within shouting distance both spoke at once. Steam puffed out of their mouths.

He stopped a scant foot in front of her and started to laugh. "We look like smoke-eaters," he said.

"Or polar bears. Oh, Zane, I'm so glad to see you!"

He said nothing, just stepped forward and wrapped his arms around her. She spoke, but her voice was muffled against his overcoat. Then she raised her face and smiled at him.

"I am dizzy with the altitude again. But this time my corset is not so tight because I do hate your smelling salts!"

"Good," was all he could say.

She rubbed her gloved hands together. "Out here in the West you have weather that is too hot and weather that is too cold. Is there nothing in between?"

"Yes, we have fall. But you went away before that. And spring is nice. Just right for swimming."

She laughed. "You mean you don't swim now, in the ice and snow?"

"Only if I've had too much hard cider." In one hand he hoisted her valise—larger this time—and grasped her elbow with the other, steering her toward the waiting buggy.

When they arrived at the house Zane walked her to the front door, then drove the buggy around back to the barn. Sam met her with Rosemarie in his arms.

"Welcome back, missy." He held the baby out to her.

Her heart stuttered as she gathered her niece in her arms.

"Oh, you've grown so big! And teeth! Let me look—why, you have three, no, four front teeth."

"Another come soon," Sam announced with a dimpled grin. "Much smart baby. Chew on toes."

Winifred buried her nose in the child's soft neck and breathed in the sweet scent of her skin. "Now that I am here, little one, you can chew on my fingers. Would you like that, my darling girl? Would you?"

"Of course she would," a masculine voice said. "She even likes *my* fingers, which must taste of alcohol or iodine."

Sam whisked her valise upstairs and Zane helped her out of the heavy winter coat, laid it over the banister and turned to her. "Are you hungry? Or thirsty?"

"Both," she said.

"A sandwich? Or some hot soup? There's leftover tomato soup from dinner and some cold chicken." He shucked his own coat while he spoke and laid it over hers.

"Both," she said again. "Oh, it is so good to be here!"

He lifted Rosemarie out of her arms and propped her against his shoulder. "Where did you get that hat, if I may ask?" He reached out and ruffled the dark fur.

"From a fancy store in downtown St. Louis. Do you like it?" She took it off and offered it to him.

"Makes you look like a Russian Cossack."

"*Da.*" She gave him a mock salute.

He laughed. "March," he ordered. "To the table." He took the chair opposite her, the baby nodding against his shoulder. "Sam," he said, when the houseboy padded down the stairs. "Could you warm up the soup?"

She felt giddy all of a sudden. From the altitude? From the enveloping warmth in the room? From...

Oh, Lord. She dared not think what the cause might be.

Sam set a bowl of steaming tomato soup before her, then brought chunks of warm bread and a plate of butter. "Make chocolate cake, too. And special cookies."

"Why, Sam, I didn't know you could make cakes."

"Bride come day after tomorrow." He beamed with such joy Winifred prayed that whoever the girl turned out to be she would be deserving of this unusual man.

Zane chuckled. "I never saw a more nervous groom. Unless," he added with a sigh, "it was me, when I married your sister."

As Winifred watched, the smile on his face faded, replaced by an odd, puzzled expression.

"You eloped with Cissy, as I recall. She never told me where you were married."

"In the chapel at the medical college. She was afraid to tell you beforehand."

Winifred said nothing. Cissy must have been blinded by love. "Were you happy, Zane?" The question popped out before she could think.

"Yes," he said simply.

All at once she felt drained. Four days on the train had tired her more than she realized. "Sam?" she called. "Could you make me some tea and bring it up to my room?"

"Try the mint tea," Zane murmured. He shifted a fussing Rosemarie to his other shoulder. "Bring her some mint tea," he called to the kitchen. "And it's time for Rosemarie's bottle."

She preceded Zane up the stairs to the same room she had occupied last summer, and Zane disappeared into his adjacent bedroom with Rosemarie. No doubt the bassinet still rested by his bed. Heat spread through her chest like warm molasses. Zane had loved Cissy. And he loved his daughter.

Rosemarie had four new teeth, she marveled. And Sam was bringing a new bride all the way from China! Life moved on. And she...well, she was playing seven concerts this coming year and increasing her teaching hours. She would be so busy she wouldn't have time to think, but it was the life she had wanted.

She sank down onto the yellow quilt and closed her eyes. Her life at the St. Louis conservatory and on the concert stage was what she'd dreamed of ever since she was five years old and playing on her first piano. And later, with Cissy, they planned for such exciting things—concerts abroad and tours throughout the United States.

Sam tapped on the door, set a tea tray on the dresser and stole into the hallway as silent as a shadow. Then she heard Zane's bedroom door open and a happy gurgle from Rosemarie.

*Oh, Cissy, I am so sorry you are missing this. So very, very sorry. You gave up so much to be with Zane, and then bear his daughter. If there is a heaven, dearest sister, I hope more than anything that you are at peace.*

The next morning Winifred found herself studying the dining room, then moving into the library and assessing it as well. Nothing suggested that it was Christmas, not a decorated tree, no festive ribbons festooning the doorways or winding up the banister, not even a single sprig of holly. She had brought presents, but there was no Christmas tree to put them under. She decided to do something about it.

After breakfast she asked Sam to find a tree she could decorate.

"Will ask sawmill man," he said. "Bring in afternoon."

Sure enough, during Rosemarie's nap, the Chinese man dragged a fragrant Douglas fir into the library and set it up on a wooden stand. Winifred stared at it for a full half hour before deciding how to adorn the bare branches.

That afternoon, while Zane was at the hospital, she paid a visit to the dressmaker, Verena Forester, and returned with seven yards of red ribbon. Quickly she cut it into short lengths and tied pretty red bows onto each tree branch. When she finished, it looked so beautiful her throat hurt.

Then she fashioned a lacy star from four white paper doilies and spread a red tablecloth beneath the tree. On top she laid the gaily wrapped presents she had brought from St. Louis.

"Much pretty," Sam observed, then turned a worried look on her. "Boss won't like."

True, Zane might not appreciate it, but she didn't care. Rosemarie would love it!

At supper that evening Zane didn't say a word about the tree until she asked him about it point blank. "Do you like the Christmas tree I decorated?"

"What tree?"

"In the library. Go look."

He returned a few moments later, his eyes shiny. "That was good of you, Winifred. Celeste had boxes of fancy ornaments stored up in the attic, but I never liked them much. And after she— Well, I like your red ribbons. Very original."

His words brought a rush of heat into her chest.

If she didn't know better she'd think she was moved by his approval.

But she *did* know better. Winifred Von Dannen was too old to be moved by Christmas trees or red ribbons or a busy physician's approval or anything else. Still, she found herself smiling at him.

And later, when Rosemary gurgled and pointed a finger at her creation, Winifred felt her own eyes fill with tears.

Zane drove Sam to the station to meet the train bringing his houseboy's new bride. They arrived two hours early because Sam was fidgeting so much he kept the house in an uproar and Zane couldn't stand it any longer. The houseboy had changed Rosemarie's perfectly dry diaper twice, spent an hour combing and rebraiding the long black queue that hung down his back, pressed and re-pressed every dress Winifred had brought with her and even steamed her green velvet gown and hung it in the empty hall closet, so nothing would wrinkle it. Unconcerned by all the bustle, the kitten curled in the corner, asleep.

Now, even bundled in a wool cape Sam had unearthed from a mysterious box he kept under his bed, the Chinese man shook in the frosty air. It was three in the afternoon and still the ground sparkled with frost.

At last the train from Portland pulled in and with a yelp Sam leaped from the buggy and raced onto the station platform.

Zane followed at a discreet distance.

Travelers stepped off the passenger car and one by one were whisked away or drifted into the station house to get out of the cold. But there was no sign of a young Chinese woman. Sam jigged from one foot to the other, squinting at the crowd.

"You think she maybe get lost?" The crestfallen houseboy clasped his arms across his body. "Maybe she not come?"

The locomotive gave a prolonged whistle and began to roll on down the track. Sam looked at Zane, his black eyes anguished.

"Not come," he said softly. He turned away, wringing his hands.

But across the tracks stood a small figure dressed in a high-collared yellow jacket and baggy black trousers. A piece of white paper was pinned to her chest, but Zane was too far away to read what it said.

"Sam," he said slowly. "Look."

Sam pivoted, his gaze following Zane's pointing finger.

The man's eyes grew wide and then the most beatific smile broke over his face. He lifted one hand toward the girl and started across the tracks.

Zane stayed put. He'd let them meet for the first time with no onlookers. He watched Sam stop before the girl, bow low and say something.

She looked up and Zane caught his breath. Sam's bride was exquisite, slim as a reed with straight black hair and skin like alabaster. The top of her head reached just to Sam's chin.

Then the Chinese man Zane thought he knew so well surprised him. Sam stepped forward and scooped his bride up into his arms, then made his way carefully across the tracks to where Zane waited.

"Slippers thin," he explained. "Not good for cold, so I carry."

He spoke a few words in Chinese and the girl nodded at Zane. The sign pinned to her blouse read "Dougherty. Smoke River."

"This is Yan Li," Sam said, his voice reverent.

Zane inclined his head and led the way to the buggy. Sam deposited Yan Li onto the seat, then stripped off his cloak and wrapped it around her. He sat shivering as the horse trotted all the way up the hill to the house.

When they arrived, Sam leaped to the ground, motioned Yan Li to the edge of the buggy seat and snatched her up once again. He carried his bride up the porch steps and into the house. Zane remembered carrying Celeste the same way.

Winifred had hot water ready for tea and some soup warming on the stove. Sam set his burden down in the front hall and lifted the cloak away from the slim figure.

"Yan Li," he said proudly. He spoke words to the girl and Winifred caught her own name, which she carefully pronounced aloud.

Yan Li lifted her gaze to Winifred's and smiled. My heavens, she was a beauty! "You have done well, Sam. Your bride is lovely."

Sam beamed and translated her words.

"She must be starving," Winifred said. The girl was probably too terrified to get off the train and purchase food at the stops along the way. What a brave thing to do, board a ship and travel thousands of miles from her home to a new country, and a new life with a man she had never seen before.

"Sam, tell her I am glad she has come."

Sam chattered to Yan Li in his own language.

"Now tell her she is safe here." Sam translated and was met by a spate of Chinese from the girl's lips.

"She say happy to be here. Not want to marry old merchant in village."

Winifred laughed softly. "Tell her she is most fortunate to come here and marry a fine man."

Zane burst into the hallway. "And for God's sake, Sam, feed her!"

Sam bustled Yan Li into the kitchen and seated her at the small table while he poured a cup of tea and began ladling the thick potato soup into a bowl. The white kitten pounced on the tassels dangling from his black slippers.

"We marry tomorrow," he said to Zane. "In church. Both Christian. But tonight, not proper to be together."

"We have another guest room, Sam. Yan Li can sleep there. I'll take her travel bag up now." He lifted the girl's small sack and headed upstairs.

Winifred sought Sam's eyes. "Is that all she brought with her?"

He spoke a few words to Yan Li. "She say that all she own. Mother's wedding dress inside and sleeping robe. Family very poor in China."

Winifred made a note to herself to visit the dressmaker and arrange for more clothes for the girl. Surely Verena Forester could sew Chinese garments? They were a thousand times more simply cut than the ruffles and bows American women were wearing these days.

As the girl spooned up her soup and Sam danced about the kitchen waiting on her it began to grow dark outside. Night came early in winter, and Winifred's apprehension began to gnaw at her.

Tonight she and Zane would drive out to the Jensens' farm for a Christmas dance. Zane thought

Sam and his bride should get to know each other with no one else around, and besides, Zane said he'd been asked to attend.

But a dance? Surely she had no place at a gathering of Zane's friends and neighbors. She knew no one except for Rooney Cloudman, the man who had left those yellow roses on Cissy's grave, and Rita at the restaurant next to the Smoke River Hotel. And the only formal dress she'd brought was the green velvet hanging in the hall closet. It had a bodice that buttoned up to her neck and long sleeves with no lace at the cuffs. She wondered what women out West wore to a dance.

The Jensens' barn was lit up like a palace, with candles in tin cans illuminating the path to the wide barn door and kerosene lamps suspended on ropes from the rafters inside. The place glowed with soft light and a potbellied woodstove in one corner made the cavernous space toasty warm.

Children raced around the perimeter of the sanded and waxed plank floor playing tag, and the men were lined up at the refreshment table, two sawhorses with cloth-covered two-by-sixes spanning them.

What women wore, Winifred soon learned, was everything under the sun. Silk with ruffles and bouncy bustles, satin with floppy bows around the hem, even wool challis cut so low in front Winifred blanched. If the wearer took one deep breath, she'd pop right out!

"What's funny?" Zane asked at her elbow.

"Nothing. Just…things are certainly different out here."

"Not so different. People talk and drink and dance and gossip just like they do back East." He opened his mouth to say more, but a manicured hand grabbed his forearm.

"Why, Zane! I didn't know you would be here tonight."

The young woman ignored Winifred and hung onto Zane's arm. "I'm free for the first reel," she said. Her voice was high-pitched, almost shrill. Whether it was that unmusical sound or the woman's proprietary attitude, Winifred's skin prickled.

Zane detached his arm from the woman's grasp. "Darla, this is Winifred Von Dannen, Celeste's sister. Winifred, Mrs. Darla Bledsoe."

Darla turned narrowed eyes on her and again grasped Zane's arm. "Oh, yes, the old maid sister. I heard about her last summer."

Winifred blinked at her rudeness. "I am pleased to meet—"

"Come on, Zane. The reel is starting." Darla pulled him away across the floor and pushed him into place just as the fiddles started up.

"Don't waste much time, does she?" said a deep voice at her elbow. Winifred turned to face the gray-haired man with the yellow roses.

"Rooney Cloudman," he reminded with a smile.

"Yes, I remember. How are you, Mr. Cloudman?"

"Make it just Rooney, why don'tcha? 'Mister' makes me nervous, like someone's gonna arrest me for somethin'."

Winifred couldn't help laughing.

"Come on over and meet my Sarah, Miss Winifred. We're gettin' married come summer." Rooney guided her to the sideline benches where a handsome older woman sat talking to a young boy.

"Sarah, this here's Winifred Von Dannen, Celeste Dougherty's sister."

Sarah smiled. "Why, my stars, you're the spitting image of her, 'cept you're dark-haired and a mite more of a real beauty."

Winifred gulped. More of a beauty? More than Cissy?

Surely the woman peering up at her had very poor eyesight.

"This here's my grandson, Mark." Sarah poked the adolescent boy in the ribs and he bolted to his feet.

"Ma'am."

Rooney touched her elbow. "Care for some cider?"

"Why, yes, I would, thank you."

"Hard or soft?"

"I beg your pardon?"

"He means distilled or just apple juice," Mark volunteered.

"Either," Winifred replied. She had no idea what the difference was.

The boy bent toward his grandmother. "Gran, can I go see if Manette will dance with me?"

"Sure ya can. Be on your best behavior, now," she said to his retreating back. Then Sarah patted the now empty space beside her.

"Set a spell with me, Winifred. I've got somethin' to say."

Winifred settled herself beside Sarah, but before she could ask what was on the older woman's mind, she caught sight of Darla Bledsoe and Zane across the room. Darla hung on him as if she had wobbly shoes and extremely poor balance. A dart of something hot and sharp stung next to her heart.

"Ah," Sarah said. "You're seein' what I see."

"It's really none of my business," Winifred said quickly.

"Or mine, either," Sarah huffed. "But I ask you, doesn't that look like a fishhook bein' dangled before that man?"

Winifred stifled a laugh just as Rooney returned

and folded her hand around a cup of something. "It's hard," he said. "All outta soft."

Winifred took a sip and gasped.

"Drink it slow-like," he advised. "Now, Sarah, you promised to teach me the two-step, so come on." He helped the older woman to her feet and guided her onto the dance floor.

Winifred gingerly sipped her cider and watched Zane. He caught her gaze from across the floor and rolled his eyes when Darla wasn't looking. At that, she lifted her cup and downed a large swallow without choking.

Then she saw something she didn't expect. Zane said something to Darla, and she hesitated, then twined her arms about his neck.

Well! And in public, too. What bad manners they had out here in the West.

But Zane lifted the clinging arms away, grasped Darla's elbow and propelled her to a seat on the sidelines. With a curt nod, he left her and strode across the floor to Winifred.

Without a word he lifted the cup of cider from her hand and downed it in one gulp. He didn't even blink.

"It's hard," she warned.

"Good."

"Would you like—?"

"Yes," he said. He marched off and in a few moments brought back her cup, filled to the brim, and another for himself.

"It's hard," he said.

"Are you referring to the cider?"

"I am not." And then they both laughed.

Zane gulped from his cup. "It's hard being a widower in a town with so many hungry young women," he explained. "Darla is a widow, so I guess she's extra-hungry. Husband was killed in a logging accident."

Winifred sipped her cider in silence. For a winter night, and sitting so far from the woodstove in the corner, it was surprising how warm she felt.

Zane plunked his empty cup onto the bench beside him, plucked hers out of her hand and pulled her to her feet.

"Dance with me."

She opened her mouth to protest but he snaked one arm around her waist and swung her onto the plank floor. "Watch out for knotholes," he said.

The music—two fiddles and a guitar, an accordion and a washtub bass—had slowed down after the lively opening reels.

Zane held her at arm's length, his hand warm at the small of her back, his soft humming barely audible. The song was "Lorena," a tune that always made her cry.

His fingers wrapped over hers and he pulled her

closer, so close his breath ruffled the escaping curls over her ear. He smelled of cider and wood smoke. She closed her eyes and let herself float in his arms until she fancied her feet had lifted off the floor.

When the music stopped they just stood there together for a moment, and then she felt Zane jerk as a hand glommed onto his forearm.

"Well, aren't you sweet to be so nice to your sister-in-law, Zane. Come on, now, it's my turn." Darla tugged at him. "It's time for the grand march and the Virginia reel. You promised."

"I did not promise," he said evenly.

"Oh, but—"

"And as you can see, Darla, I am engaged at the moment."

Without another word he swung Winifred back onto the dance floor.

"I think," she ventured when he had danced her to the opposite side of the room, "there might be a better way to tame a tiger."

"I don't want to tame her."

"I meant," Winifred said carefully, "to keep from being eaten."

Zane laughed at that, stopped dancing and looked Winifred full in the face. "I do not want to remarry."

"Perhaps that is not what Darla has in mind, Zane."

He gave her a long look. "That, too, I do not want." He said nothing more, just held her in silence and moved them about the floor.

She felt too hot, then cold, then too warm again. He was humming along with the music again, this time a tune she did not recognize. It was in waltz time, but they kept dancing a slow two-step, as before, close enough for her to feel the heat from his body, close enough to brush his chin with her lips if she turned her head. They did not talk, and then as his arm tightened across her back she could think of nothing to say.

She thought of all the young men she had known since she had come of age, men from prominent families with brilliant music careers ahead of them; men who tossed bouquets at her over the footlights and introduced themselves over supper; men who begged for her attention, who cosseted and flattered and talked romantic nonsense.

But she had never before felt like this when she was with a man, as if her body were full of stars and a fire smoldered deep inside her. With a low laugh she tipped her head back and found Zane looking at her, his gray eyes darkened almost to charcoal.

"What is it?" she whispered. "You have such an odd look on your face, what are you thinking?"

"To be honest, I don't really know. Ask me instead about the fiddle players or why Sarah Rose's grandson can waltz better than I can. Or," he said in a lower tone, "what I am feeling at this moment."

"I cannot ask you that, Zane. What you are feeling is none of my business."

The musicians struck up a Virginia reel and Zane steered Winifred over to join the other dancers. The line of couples advanced toward each other, bowed and moved back. Then the lead couple joined hands and circled around each other.

Zane watched his sister-in-law's graceful form skip forward, then back, then forward again to meet him in the center and slide-step all the way to the end. Her eyes shone. Laughter lit up her face as if candles burned beneath her skin. She was gorgeous in that green dress. She was intoxicating.

She was life itself, and he knew every man in the room wanted her.

*He* wanted her. He stumbled, missed a step, then two before he could recover. Goodness, he must be drunk.

He watched her join hands with Wash Halliday and spin around in the center, then spin with Thad MacAllister, and a bolt of pure male possessiveness shot through him.

He was not drunk, he realized. He was stone-cold sober and he was feeling like any normal male, fiercely, agonizingly jealous.

What an irony. At last he was coming back to life after Celeste's death, but the cruel joke God was playing on him made him grind his teeth. He couldn't desire his sister-in-law. There was something in the Bible about it, but at the moment he couldn't remember what it was.

After the set, Wash Halliday introduced Winifred to his wife, Jeanne, and then to Thad and Leah MacAllister. The five of them chatted for longer than Zane thought he could stand, but then Winifred's gaze strayed around the room, searching for him.

He started toward her but once again found himself waylaid by Darla Bledsoe.

"Zane, you promised to dance with me again," she pleaded.

He could have refused but it would be rude, and he suspected Darla could be spiteful. He offered his arm and with a triumphant grin she swept him onto the plank dance floor.

Over Darla's shoulder he saw Winifred partnered with first Charlie Kincaid, then Seth Ruben and then the barber, Whitey Poletti. And then he lost track. Rooney Cloudman, dancing a spirited varsouvienne with Sarah Rose, accidentally bumped into him, and when Zane righted himself, he heard Rooney's voice at his back.

"She'll get away if yer not careful."

Zane shot a look at the older man but was met with such a poker face he had to chuckle. He knew exactly what Rooney meant.

Darla tugged his lapel. "What?"

"Nothing. Just a moment of clarity." He knew she wouldn't understand and he sure as hell would not explain.

Long past midnight the musicians packed up their instruments and parents gathered up sleeping children. Darla swished over to where Zane stood at the refreshment table waiting for Winifred to say good-night to the MacAllisters and Sarah Rose.

"Why, Zane, isn't that mistletoe I see over the barn door?"

"It is. Pretty, isn't it? Deadly poison, though. I'd stay away from it."

He broke away and went to meet Winifred, just coming across the room toward him. She smiled up into his face.

"Oh, I've had such a good time," she said. "I didn't expect to enjoy myself at all. I met so many nice people. Did you know Sarah Rose is getting married next June? And Seth Ruben just bought the lumber company?"

Zane draped her long black coat about her shoulders. "Yes, I did, and no, I didn't." He shrugged into his overcoat. "Wait here, Winifred. I'll bring the buggy around."

*And don't talk to any more single men.*

## *Chapter Eight*

Winifred waited for Zane to come in the back door from the barn. Sam had left a lantern burning low in the entry hall, and there wasn't a sound in the house but the crackle of the fireplace in the dining room, which sent out a comforting heat after the chilly ride home. Winifred slipped off her coat and hung it away in the closet.

She was warming her hands at the hearth when Zane tramped in. "Come over by the fire," she invited.

He dropped his heavy coat over the banister. "Everyone asleep?"

"Yes, even Rosemarie, I think. At least I don't hear her crying."

He set the lantern on the stairway and joined her in front of the fireplace. "I watched you tonight," he said.

"I know. I wondered why."

"I wondered myself," he confessed.

Their eyes met. Very slowly, Zane reached out his hands and turned her toward him, then cupped her face between his hands and tipped her mouth up to meet his.

Her eyes closed when their lips met and stayed closed while his mouth moved gently over hers. When he raised his head she caught his hands in her own and lifted them away from her face.

"Zane," she whispered. "This is wrong."

"No," he said, his voice quiet. "It isn't wrong. Premature, maybe. Maybe not wise. But not wrong."

"I—"

"Go on up to bed, Winifred." He turned her toward the stairs. "Take the lamp."

For a long time after Winifred climbed the stairs Zane sat in his office in the dark, a glass of brandy at his elbow, his head in his hands. When the hall clock chimed three, he shoved the brandy aside and rose.

Moonlight flooded the hallway and he made his way up the stairs without lighting a candle, walked softly past Winifred's closed door and flung himself fully clothed across his bed.

Winifred was not asleep. How could she possibly sleep after such a night? And Zane's kiss… what had possessed him to do such an impulsive thing? Perhaps it was the hard cider he'd consumed?

Each time she closed her eyes she saw his face, grave and calm. But his eyes—oh, Lord, his eyes! In their shadowed depths she saw pain and acceptance and loneliness. And hunger.

Well, of course. He was a man, like any other man, was he not? He needed a woman.

But not Darla Bledsoe.

*And not me.*

She rolled over and then heard a soft cry. Not Rosemarie, who wailed at a different pitch when she was hungry or wet. This was stifled sobbing that drifted from the guest bedroom next to hers.

Yan Li. She sprang out of bed and tiptoed next door, tapped once and walked in. The girl was sitting on the bed, her knees drawn up, her face buried in her hands. Winifred sank down beside her, reached out her arms and drew her close.

"There, now," she crooned. "It's all right. Everything will be all right."

She knew Sam's bride couldn't tell her what was wrong, so she just smoothed her hand over the thick black hair and rocked the shaking girl.

After a long while Yan Li lifted her head and tried to smile. But in the moon's light Winifred could see her mouth tremble and her cheeks glistened as fat tears rolled down and dripped onto her neck.

"Yan Li, watch my hand." Winifred forked two fingers and walked them across the quilt. With her other hand she formed another set of legs and moved them until they mashed together. Then she looked at Yan Li with a question.

"Is that it? You do not want to marry Wing Sam?"

The girl caught on instantly. She formed her own set of legs and brushed Winifred's left hand aside, then walked her fingers around and around the remaining set of legs. She looked up expectantly.

"Of course," Winifred said. "You like Wing Sam. It is the thought of marriage that frightens you. And you have no mother to calm your fears."

She laid her free hand over the girl's fingers and nodded. "It will be all right, Yan Li. I promise." She hugged the slim form, gently pressed her down onto the pillow and smoothed her damp cheek. "It will be all right," she whispered.

Halfway through breakfast the following morning, the doorbell clanged. Zane threw his napkin down onto the dining table and rose. "Jupiter, it's Christmas Day. Nobody gets sick on Christmas Day."

But it was not a patient. Before him in the doorway stood Leah MacAllister.

"I rode in from the ranch this morning because last night at the dance Winifred asked me to come for your houseboy, Sam's sake. You see, I speak Chinese."

Zane knew Leah MacAllister was half-Chinese, the niece of the bakery owner Uncle Charlie, whose fan-tan losses had partly paid for Yan Li's passage to Portland.

"Come in, Leah." He took her coat and wool scarf and gloves just as Winifred stepped into the hallway.

"Oh, Leah, thank you for coming into town on Christmas morning. I was right, we do need you."

The two women brushed past Zane and he sat down to finish his breakfast, listening to the women's voices in the kitchen speaking the same strange-sounding language Sam did until Winifred joined him. A smile played around her mouth and she shot him a significant look from across the table.

"Was I not clever to ask Leah MacAllister to come? Poor Yan Li has no one to calm her wedding jitters, certainly not Sam."

Zane could only nod. The unspoken bond between women sometimes amazed him.

Winifred smiled. "There are times when a

woman wants to confide in another woman. Cissy used to confide in me until—"

She broke off.

"Until she met me," Zane supplied. "She often said how much she missed you."

"But she never wrote," Winifred said in surprise.

"She was afraid to. She felt you were angry with her."

Winifred looked away. "I was angry," she said quietly. "I could not understand how she could throw away her musical career, and mine along with it. I was very angry."

"Are you still angry?"

"I was for a long time. Cissy and I were the Von Dannen sisters, duo piano artists. After she ran away with you, I had to become a soloist. It was a difficult transition."

"And now?"

She looked into his eyes. "Now I am beginning to understand how she could give it all up. She fell in love with you, and when that happened, I no longer mattered."

A peal of girlish laughter sounded from the kitchen. A moment later Sam poked his head into the dining room. "Wedding two o'clock, Boss. You come?"

Zane snorted. "Of course I will come, Sam. It isn't every day a man gets married."

Sam grinned and disappeared into the kitchen.

"Or a woman," Winifred added. "Just think how Yan Li must feel this morning."

"Scared to death," Zane acknowledged. "I'll wager Sam is, too. I'm going to hitch up the buggy so Sam can drive Yan Li to the church. I can walk. It's just down the hill."

"Wait," Winifred cried. "I shipped a wedding gift for Sam from St. Louis. Did it arrive?"

"It did. It fits nicely on the new double bed I gave them. Sam's bed was too narrow for—" He swallowed and Winifred released a bubble of laughter.

"Why, Dr. Dougherty, you're blushing!"

"I am not blushing," he insisted.

Winifred choked back a challenge. Perhaps Zane would not appreciate her teasing. She wondered how he had withstood Cissy's penchant for teasing, something Winifred clearly recalled from their girlhood. But of course Zane had loved Cissy, and she supposed a man in love would put up with a great deal.

Zane left for the barn. Then tall, russet-haired Thad MacAllister arrived to accompany Leah to the church. Sam appeared in a new yellow knee-length tunic embroidered in black, and Yan Li stood shyly at his side in her mother's red wedding robe and the shimmery red headdress Leah had brought for her to wear.

The young Chinese girl looked so radiant Winifred's eyes filled with tears. Sam looked at his bride as if he'd been hit over the head with a chunk of firewood. He bowed low before his bride, then took her hand and led her out the front door to the waiting buggy.

"Reminds me of when I married Leah," Thad MacAllister said to her. "I was struck dumb at the sight of her." Out of the corner of her eye Winifred saw the tall rancher whisper something to his wife and press his lips to her forehead.

Something leaped in Winifred's chest. Zane had said something like that about Cissy. *She was the most beautiful creature I had ever seen.*

Suddenly she felt left out. Something wondrous that other people experienced had passed her by. She had seen admiration in a man's eyes, but she had never seen the kind of awe she noted on Sam's face.

Resolutely she put Sam and Yan Li and Zane and Cissy out of her mind, closed the front door and went upstairs to tend to Rosemarie.

At the church altar, Sam and Yan Li joined hands and faced the shiny-faced pastor, Reverend Pollock, who stood with the Bible spread open in his hands. Leah MacAllister stood at Yan Li's left, quietly translating the minister's words.

Zane watched the ceremony with both joy and sadness. He was happy for Sam; at the same time he remembered with a dart of pain reciting those same vows with Celeste just three years before, and his chest ached. He still missed her. He would always miss her.

And her sister, Winifred? He could not bring himself to think of Winifred at this moment.

*What God hath joined together, let no man put asunder…*

*So long as you both shall live.*

It was over, and Sam and Yan Li stood hand in hand, accepting congratulations and wishes for long life. Zane shook Sam's hand and brushed a kiss across Yan Li's pale cheek.

Tonight would be her wedding night. He decided he would leave the house for a while. He wanted to take Winifred somewhere, anywhere, but he didn't suppose they could both leave. On a man's wedding night he shouldn't hear a baby crying in an upstairs bedroom and he shouldn't be expected to care for it.

When the newlywed couple had signed the register and slipped away, Zane took off himself on a long walk that ended up at the hospital, where he stayed until past midnight. On his walk back up the hill to the house he noticed it was snowing.

Winifred had wheeled the bassinet into her bedroom and was soothing a fussy Rosemarie with a lullaby when Zane came up the stairs.

"She's teething," he said from the open doorway. "Give her something cold to chew on."

"What 'something'?"

"An icicle. I'll bring up a bowlful."

A few minutes later he presented a china bowl of icicles and pulled a handkerchief from his vest pocket. "Tie some snow in the corner and let her suck on it."

"Tell me about the wedding," she asked as she knotted the fabric.

When he didn't answer, she looked up. "Was the ceremony nice?"

"Yes, it was. You know what a wedding is like—people cry."

"No, I do not know," she said carefully. "I have never been to a wedding."

Zane said nothing for a long moment, just looked at her. "After the ceremony I went to the hospital."

His eyes looked tired, and his collar was undone. He was a good man. Cissy might have rushed into marriage, but she had been fortunate in her choice. Zane was caring and dedicated. Conscientious.

And extremely handsome, she admitted. Is that what Cissy saw that night when they met? She could not have seen below the surface then, seen beneath his personable good looks to the man underneath. There had not been enough time between the recital at the medical college that night and secretly marrying him. But surely committed love relationships were not built on such ephemeral things as a pink chiffon gown and a handsome face.

Or were they? She studied him, trying to see what Cissy had really seen. It seemed to make him uncomfortable because he stood looking down at her for a long minute. "You have never attended a wedding?"

"No. Professional musicians rarely get married."

"I see." He stood a moment longer, then turned away. "Good night, Winifred."

He disappeared down the darkened hallway to his own bedroom. She tried very hard not to hear his movements through the wall as she replaced Rosemarie's now-warm teething cloth with a cold one.

The next morning Winifred brought a still fussy Rosemarie downstairs for her morning bottle and some warm applesauce Sam had prepared, then took her place at the dining room table across from a preoccupied Zane.

"Sleep all right?" he asked.

"Y-yes. The baby woke only once and dropped right off again when I rocked the bassinet and hummed a song."

"I didn't sleep. Too quiet."

Winifred stared at him. "You missed Rosemarie?"

"I did." He sent her an apologetic look. "Maybe I'm a possessive father."

Winifred laughed. "You're devoted, Zane. Not possessive."

He studied his plate. "When you love someone, you grow to be possessive."

Sam stepped in with a platter of pancakes and the coffeepot. The small rounded cakes were artfully topped with dollops of orange marmalade. "Oh, Sam, how nice."

"Yan Li make," he said proudly. "Cook good." The houseboy set down the coffeepot and levered a spatula under the pancakes, sliding six onto her plate.

A happy squeal erupted from the kitchen. "Also feed baby," Sam explained. He set the platter down in front of Zane and filled his coffee cup just as the front doorbell sounded.

Zane sighed and pushed back his chair. Then Winifred heard the door open and Zane's surprised voice.

"Darla, what—?"

Winifred's hand froze on her fork.

"Oh, Zane, I've hurt myself."

"Come in and sit here in the chair. Tell me what happened?"

"It's my foot. My toe, actually. I—I dropped something and it hit my toe."

"What did you drop?"

"The cookie jar."

Sam paused in the act of pouring Winifred's coffee and caught her eye. His black eyes twinkled.

"I'll just remove your shoe," Zane said in a patient tone. "Now roll down your stocking."

A long silence ensued. Sam lifted the coffeepot, but Winifred shook her head and put her finger to her lips. He nodded and stood motionless beside the table.

"Your little toe is red and swollen," Zane said. "Probably broken."

"Oh." She moaned dramatically. "Should you bandage it or something?"

"There's no need. It will heal on its own. Try to stay off it for a few days."

"But—"

"I'll give you some powdered willow bark to add to your tea. You can pick up more at the mercantile. By the way, how did you get up here to the house?"

"I...well, I walked."

Zane expelled a breath loud enough to be heard in the dining room. "I'll drive you home in the buggy. Put your shoe back on and wait here."

"Oh, by the way, Zane, I'm having a social at my house tomorrow after—"

"Can't make it," he said shortly. "Hospital duty."

He came through the dining room looking flushed and angry. A moment later the back door slammed.

"Boss miss breakfast," Sam whispered.

"He's a conscientious doctor." Winifred spoke quietly so Darla wouldn't hear.

"Lady trick Boss," the houseboy muttered. He poured her cup full and tipped Zane's pancakes back onto the platter.

Winifred sipped her coffee and thought about Darla Bledsoe. She didn't like the woman, but she had to admire her brash persistence. She knew from her women friends at the conservatory that many a man had succumbed to less.

But not Zane. He was not simple-minded in that way. And besides, she told herself, apparently Zane did not even *like* Darla. But what if he were... desperate?

What made a man desperate? she wondered suddenly. Didn't people marry because they cared about each other? Because they loved each other?

Cissy had swept Zane off his feet and she had fallen instantly in love with him.

Is that how it happened? Pink chiffon and penetrating deep blue eyes? Surely relationships were not built on such ephemeral things, a pink chiffon gown and a handsome face.

Or were they?

She finished her coffee and stepped into the kitchen while Sam gathered up the dishes. Yan Li looked up from the spoonful of applesauce she was offering to Rosemarie and smiled. Goodness, the girl positively glowed this morning!

Winifred quickly made the fingers of both hands into make-believe legs as she had the previous night and walked them toward each other, close enough to touch. Then she sent Yan Li a questioning look. "Is everything all right with you and Sam?"

Yan Li reached her hand out, mashed Winifred's fingers together and blushed scarlet. Then she dropped her head.

"Yan Li?"

The girl raised her face and the most wonderful smile spread across her mouth. Winifred caught her breath. Happy? The girl was ecstatic. She bent and quickly kissed the smooth cheek.

Sam, too, was unusually sunny this morning. When he entered the kitchen with the pancake platter, Winifred stopped him and kissed his cheek, too. Then stepped over the kitten and headed for the library.

From the kitchen she heard murmured words in Chinese and a burst of delighted laughter. Oh, my. For some reason, she felt like crying. What on earth was the matter with her?

She read for a while, then heard a funny thumping noise coming toward her. She looked down, and there was Rosemarie scuttling across the floor on her hands and knees with Yan Li in pursuit.

The baby crawled over to Winifred and slapped at her shoes, cooing happily. Yan Li brought the laundry basket and settled the baby into it, close enough for Winifred to jiggle it if she cried.

Which she did the minute Yan Li left the room. Not a big wail, as if she were hungry, just a little whimper of discontent. Another new tooth, maybe.

Winifred smiled at herself. She worried over Rosemarie as if she were her mother, not just her aunt. Another small cry and she scooped her niece into her arms.

She tried humming a song, but it didn't help. Next she tried singing the words. "Mama's little baby loves short'nin'…" No use. This little baby didn't love anything at all this morning.

The whimpers grew louder. In desperation Winifred rose, settled her in the laundry basket and went to the piano. At the very first chord, Rose-marie went quiet, and Winifred glanced over at the basket.

The child's blue-green eyes were wide open, her head cocked in apparent interest. Winifred's heart rolled over. "You like music, do you, little one?"

She began to play, first a Brahms waltz, then another, and all the while Rosemarie cooed and gurgled with happiness.

Zane returned from driving Darla home, stepped quietly into the library and stopped short. His baby daughter was staring at Winifred at the piano with such absorption he had to chuckle.

Winifred broke off midphrase. "Oh! I didn't hear you come in."

"For God's sake, don't stop playing. You seem to have discovered a cure for teething babies!" He plucked Rosemarie out of the basket and settled her on his lap in the upholstered wingback chair by the fireplace.

"You don't mind my playing the piano? I mean playing pieces that Cissy must have played?"

"I don't, no. You play differently. And I've missed the music since Celeste—since she died." He brought the baby to his shoulder, leaned back in the chair and closed his eyes.

Winifred turned back to the keyboard. An hour later when she looked up, Zane was sound asleep with Rosemarie slumbering peacefully against his chest. She left them there and tiptoed into the kitchen to ask Sam to make a fresh pot of coffee and some toast for Zane when he woke up.

## Chapter Nine

Winifred sighed and rolled over in her bed when a persistent tap at her bedroom door woke her. The door opened and Zane wheeled in the bassinet with Rosemarie snuggled under the pink flannel coverlet.

"Winifred, I have an emergency. My nurse, Elvira Sorensen, has been shot."

"Shot!" Winifred sat straight up. "Who shot her?"

Zane blew out a long breath. "Her husband. He's in the jail now. Marshal Johnson will take him to Boise in the morning."

"Oh, Zane. Will she live?"

"I don't know. I'll try my damnedest." He bent to kiss the baby and quietly closed the door behind him.

Zane did not leave the hospital for the next thirty-six hours. Elvira lay in a coma, the bullet lodged so deep in her breast he couldn't risk prob-ing for it until she was stable. If she made it at all. He sat at her bedside, paced up and down the hall, consulted with his partner, gray-haired Samuel Graham and sweated out the hours.

"Let's wait another twelve hours, Zane," Samuel said. "See if she regains consciousness."

"Hard to do, Samuel. Every hour that passes she gets weaker. If we went in now, at least she wouldn't feel it."

"If we went in now, she might never feel any-thing ever again. Go home, Zane. Get some sleep."

"Can't. I'll stay with her till morning."

"I'll stop by your house on my way home and let them know you'll be late." The older man turned to go.

"Oh, Samuel? Would you ask my houseboy if he'd bring some of those pancakes his wife makes?"

An hour later, Winifred arrived carrying a bas-ket of warm pancakes and a quart jar of hot coffee wrapped in flannel. Her hat and long black coat were dusted with snow.

Zane stepped past Elvira's hospital room and took the basket. "Snowing again?"

"Just started. How is Mrs. Sorensen?"

"Fighting hard."

"Will she—?"

"Don't know. Can't operate yet. Winifred, thanks for the coffee and the food. Now go on back to the house. No use your getting your toes and fingers frozen."

Winifred looked at him oddly, then stretched up on tiptoe to brush a kiss against his cheek.

He stared at her, wondering if he'd dreamed what just happened. "What's that for?"

"I don't know. I just felt… I don't know."

As tired as he was, Zane smiled. "You're one helluva puzzling woman, Winifred."

She blushed crimson and turned away.

"Winifred."

She halted but did not turn toward him. "One helluva woman," he said again. "Thanks."

Hours later, Zane stumbled through his front door so tired he could scarcely see and so drained his mind couldn't focus. Sam met him at the bottom of the staircase, a plate in his hand.

"You hungry, Boss?"

"Hell, I don't know. What meal is next?"

"Breakfast. You miss supper."

Zane ran his hands through his hair. "It's still dark outside. Got any coffee?"

"Make fast. Toast, too."

"Just coffee. Bring it upstairs, could you?"

"Right away, Boss."

"Is everyone asleep?"

"Baby in Missy Winifred's room, but she wait up for you."

For some reason Sam's words spread warmth into his chest but he was too exhausted to analyze why. He tramped up the stairs to his bedroom, threw himself across the quilt and laid his arm across his eyes. He heard the tap on his door and it swung open.

"Leave it on the nightstand, Sam. And leave the lamp on downstairs and the door open. I don't want to light a candle. Afraid I'll knock it over. And thanks, Sam."

"It isn't Sam, Zane. It's me." Winifred sat down on the bed beside him. "How is Mrs. Sorensen?"

"Alive. We got the bullet out. I'd like to shoot her husband for putting her through this."

Sam slipped in and quietly set a tray of coffee and toast on the nightstand. When he left, Winifred started to rise, but Zane reached out his hand and grasped her arm. "Stay. Please."

He felt her stiffen, and without thinking he wrapped both arms around her. "Don't go."

"I must, Zane. It's very late, and I—"

"Please." He pulled her forward and splayed his fingers on her bare neck. He guessed she had on a night robe of some sort—it felt silky. She smelled of soap and lemons.

His hand moved to the hairpins holding her

coiled braids in place; slowly he began to slip them free, then unbound the braids and combed his fingers through the thick waves.

"Zane," she said softly. "Stop. You're so tired you aren't thinking clearly."

"I know exactly what I'm doing."

"You're exhausted. And you need to eat something. Here, have some toast."

"I'd rather have this. You."

She jerked upright.

He groaned. "Forget it. You're right, I'm not thinking clearly. I hardly know what I'm saying."

She broke off a piece of toast and poked it past his lips. "Eat." Obediently he chewed and swallowed.

"It's been an awful night, Winifred."

She offered another piece of toast, and then another, and raised his head for a sip of coffee.

"More," he murmured. When she replaced the cup on the tray he pulled her down until her breasts grazed his shirt. "Winifred, don't go. Not yet." He smoothed his hands down her silk-swathed arms and felt her tremble. With a small sound she lay down beside him on the quilt, and he found himself thanking God he had a bed wide enough for two.

If he had the energy, he'd rip off her nightgown, but he didn't. Instead he just held her and wondered vaguely what the hell he was doing.

She said nothing, and after a while he heard the door close and the dark envelop them. The last thing he remembered was her scent and her soft breathing at his side.

Hours later when he awoke she was gone. Of course. In God's name, what had he been thinking?

The gray light outside the window told him it was already dawn. The baby must be fed and changed, apologies made to Winifred.

He gritted his teeth and rolled away from the light. He couldn't face any of it just yet. He shucked the rest of his clothes, gulped the now-cold coffee and ate the last slice of toast. Then he crawled beneath the quilt and closed his eyes.

Zane slept around the clock. Winifred kept the baby downstairs with her so her hungry cries would not wake him. Sam retrieved the tray of coffee and Yan Li made more for her breakfast. Both of them urged Winifred to eat something, but she couldn't.

She'd spent half the night beside Zane, but she knew he would never remember any of it, or the things he had said. He'd been up two straight nights; he must have been only half-conscious.

With a start she plunked down her coffee cup. *She* would never forget any of it. She would never forget how she felt when Zane touched her skin, unpinned her hair. She'd felt shaky inside, and so happy it was…it was like a strange and beautiful dream.

She must not feel such things for this man! He was her sister's husband, her brother-in-law. Such relationships were impossible.

Late in the morning Zane finally came downstairs, his shirt rumpled and his uncombed dark hair falling into his eyes.

Winifred heard his voice from the library where she sat on the floor next to Rosemarie in her basket.

"Sam?"

"You call, Boss?"

"Any coffee left?"

"Oh, yes. Fresh pot. Also good eggs Yan Li cook."

Zane collapsed into a dining chair and let Sam and Yan Li fuss over him. Winifred had breakfasted hours ago, but she came in from the library and sat down across from him.

"Dr. Graham stopped in an hour ago. He says Mrs. Sorensen is doing well."

Zane nodded. "I'd still like to shoot that sonofa—"

He broke off as the doorbell rang. Sam streaked to the entry hall, and Winifred heard his voice, then the voice of Charlie Kincaid, the stationmaster.

"Telegram for Miss Von Dannen."

Winifred half rose from her chair as Sam laid it in her hand. She ripped it open with shaking fingers and felt the blood drain from her head.

Zane looked up. "What is it?"

"Millicent, my fellow professor at the conservatory—she has had an accident. Her wrist is broken and she has committed to a concert in ten days. She wants me to play in her place."

"Can you do that? Just step in at the last minute?"

"I—I will have to try. But it means I must return to St. Louis as soon as possible."

"There's a train for the East every day at noon," Zane said. "I'll drive you to the station."

Winifred was packed and ready in an hour. Leaving this time was more difficult than she'd expected. Sam pressed a packet of cheese and cold chicken into her hand, and Yan Li hugged her, sniffing back tears.

But the worst part was Rosemarie, who cried and clung to her neck until Yan Li pried her arms free and cuddled her against her shoulder.

Winifred closed the front door against the baby's wails and walked resolutely down the porch steps. Everything in her screamed "stay," but of course she could not. She had professional obligations to fulfill.

And there was something else. While she

adored her niece, she knew she had no business being in Zane's life.

He handed her into the buggy and wrapped a fur robe about her knees. They rode in silence down the hill to the station, and he went inside to purchase her ticket.

She watched his tall form disappear into the station house and felt a queer heaviness settle under her breastbone. He was a good man. A wonderful man.

She would miss him.

They waited for the train without speaking. As before, Zane paced up the tracks and back, his hands jammed in the pockets of his overcoat, the wind ruffling his dark hair. Each time he returned to her side he held her gaze, his gray eyes somber.

At last the locomotive whistle sounded. Winifred started forward, but Zane stopped her with a hand on her arm. "Winifred, about last night…"

"It's all right, Zane. I understand. You were exhausted, and I—"

He shook his head. "You don't understand. I remember everything I did, everything I said. I meant every word."

"Zane—"

"Oh, God, Winifred, don't stop me or I'll never get this said. I—I care about you."

"Of course. I know you do. I am Celeste's sister."

"No, dammit, that's not what I mean." He curled his hands about her upper arms. "That's not all of it."

She looked up into a face tense with unspoken feeling. "What, then?"

"I—"

The locomotive whistle obliterated his words. The train slid past until the passenger car rolled to the platform, and Winifred moved forward.

Zane stepped ahead of her, swung her valise onto the iron boarding step and then turned back to her. He didn't speak, just gripped her shoulders, pulled her into his arms and caught her mouth under his.

His kiss shattered her equilibrium, left her dazed and trembling and suddenly unsure of where she was or what she was doing. If his lips had moved over hers for one more second, she would never have boarded the train.

He turned her away from him and propelled her onto the iron step.

He mouthed his last words: "Come back."

January 9th

Dear Zane,

My concert is over. I did not play brilliantly, as I would have preferred, but Pierre de Fulet, the orchestra conductor, gave me a solo curtain call and afterwards I found bouquets of beautiful flowers heaped in my dressing room.

Poor Millicent is having a difficult time with her broken wrist. It is not healing well, and I am taking all her piano students for the new term. I am also filling in for her on two more concert engagements. Heavens, I am feeling tired already.

The snow has not let up for a single day since my return. My students arrive half-frozen and only after massive doses of hot chocolate do their fingers thaw enough to play a decent scale. Unfortunately, my upcoming performances are at least one day's journey farther east, and the trains are abominably heated. If you are fortunate enough to sit near the stove, you won't freeze, but otherwise the weather is miserable.

My father is not well. He is eighty-seven now, and the doctors say his heart is weakening. I try to spend as many evenings with him as I can, but with all the concerts I am playing that is not nearly often enough. It is amazing to me that he has lasted these many years since Mama died, and for a good many of those he had two rambunctious girls underfoot. Papa was forty-seven when he married Mama, and he was almost sixty when I was born.

I must close now and do some much-needed practicing of my Beethoven. His concertos are the most demanding in my repertoire.

Winifred


February 13th

Dear Winifred,

Tomorrow is Valentine's Day and the Jensens are holding another barn dance. At least it will be warmer than the last one, at Christmas. I recall wishing I had a muff such as you ladies wear!

Sam's kitten has grown into a sleek, over-fed, much-petted creature that is absolutely terrified of mice. The best-laid plans, etc. etc. Rosemarie has taken a great liking to the worthless puss and pets her for hours and sings songs to her.

Yan Li is rapidly learning English. Not only is she a fine cook, she is very intelligent and good-natured. No matter how many of my patients track mud into the entry hall, Yan Li never frowns. Sam worships her.

My nurse, Elvira Sorensen, is recuperating slowly but has made me promise not to replace her. She insists she will work at the hospital until her dying day. Her husband has been sent to the federal prison in Boise. Seems he was wanted for a murder in Idaho. Elvira certainly deserved better.

I suspect Rosemarie has a gift for music, as she hums and chatters songs of her own making with words that are unintelligible to all but the cat, who meows along with her and purrs when she stops. She will be walking when you return in June!

You are coming in June, are you not? Sarah Rose and Rooney Cloudman are expecting you at their wedding.

Yours, Zane

April 17th.

Dear Zane,

I have been so tired of late I cannot recall if I mailed a letter to you in March. I am more in demand for concerts and recitals than ever before, even when Cissy and I were a piano duo team. I have seven concerts between the end of this month and the end of May—three with full orchestra.

Millicent is able to teach again, but our combined students total twice as many as last year at this time. I wonder where all these young pianists are coming from?

My father is worse. I have hired a full-time nurse, and while he is in good spirits—at least he claims he is—he grows weaker by the day. It breaks my heart to see him this way, so worn and thin. I never want to grow old. Never!

I must close, as an extra rehearsal has just been called for tomorrow's performance at the new opera house.

Winifred

May 12th
Dear Zane,
My father has passed away. It is all I can do not to rail at God for taking him. Everyone at the conservatory is being very kind, and it eases somewhat the awful ache I feel inside.

The funeral is tomorrow afternoon.
Winifred

May 16th.
Dear Winifred,
You must know how much I grieve with you for your father's loss. Death is such a blow that I sometimes wonder how we human beings manage to go on with our lives. Ce-

leste's death left me numb for days. I hope this will not be true for you, for it is hell to get through.

I am thinking of you.

Zane

PS: I am still expecting you in June. Do you promise?

May 29th

Dear Winifred,

I have heard nothing from you for weeks. Are you all right?

Zane

June 7th

Dear Zane,

I have been teaching nonstop and have two more concerts before the end of the term. I plan to arrive on the seventeenth. I am so tired I will have to sleep for a week when I get there.

Winifred

## Chapter Ten

The train from St. Louis pulled into the Smoke River station with a blast of its whistle and squealing brakes. Zane tied the buggy reins to the brake handle, climbed down and strode onto the platform. He scanned the passenger car for a glimpse of Winifred through the windows, then watched the people debarking. Person after person stepped off the train but there was no sign of her.

The platform cleared. Had she missed the train? Could he have misunderstood the date? Convulsively he clenched his fists.

And then a slight figure in a pale green skirt and matching shirtwaist stepped down onto the iron step. A uniformed conductor set a valise behind her and handed her a green paisley shawl.

Her face looked flushed. She paused, holding onto the handrail for support, and Zane surged forward. "Winifred!"

He reached her just as she took an uncertain step toward him. "Zane."

And then her knees gave way and she crumpled. He caught her up into his arms. "Winifred, are you all right?"

She opened her eyes. "Valise," she murmured. "Can't lift."

He swung toward the train and nodded for the conductor to set her luggage onto the platform. "Charlie!" He yelled for the stationmaster, then halted a young boy racing toward the station house. "Get Mr. Kincaid, will you, son? Ask him to keep that valise over there behind his desk."

"Sure, Doc." The boy trotted off.

Zane carried her to the buggy, slid her onto the seat and hurriedly climbed into the driver's seat. Before he even lifted the reins, Winifred tipped over against his shoulder. Her teeth were chattering.

For the first time in his life he whipped a horse, but even so it seemed to take hours to reach the house. He reined up, set the brake and jumped out.

"Sam!"

He pulled Winifred into his arms and started up the porch steps. "Sam!"

The front door swung open ahead of him and without a word Sam reached out to help him. "Take the buggy back to the station. Get her valise from Charlie."

Inside he brushed past a wide-eyed Yan Li,
climbed the stairs two at a time and laid Winifred
on her bed in the room next to his. She was barely
conscious. Hurriedly he unbuttoned her shirtwaist,
yanked his stethoscope from his back pocket where
he always carried it and bent over her.

Her skin was too hot. Her heartbeat was thready
and irregular, but the rales he heard in her lungs
told him everything.

Her eyelids fluttered open. "Am I ill?" she whispered.

"You have pneumonia, Winifred. Both lungs."
He straightened and shouted over his shoulder.
"Yan Li. Bring a basin of cool water and some
towels."

He turned his attention back to Winifred and
finished unbuttoning her blouse. "I've got to bring
down your fever. Need to sponge you off."

She nodded. Her lids drifted shut. "Thirsty,"
she muttered.

Yan Li stepped into the room, a china basin of
water in her hands and two clean towels draped
over one arm. "Sam here now," she said.

"Ask him to bring up the valise. See if you can
find her night robe."

A soft patter of footsteps echoed down the stairs
and then returned. "Robe," Yan Li said. She laid
the silky garment across the single chair in the

room. He recognized it, the blue one with long sleeves, and his breath caught.

"Winifred, I'm going to remove your clothes and sponge you off." She nodded but her eyes remained closed.

Zane pulled her shirtwaist off her shoulders, then unlaced her corset and unbuttoned her skirt. He drew it off, along with the single lace-trimmed petticoat she wore.

"Not very romantic," she murmured.

"Don't talk."

He hesitated, then stripped off her chemise, but left on her ruffled drawers. Damn, she was beautiful. He dipped a towel in the water and laid it over her chest.

"Feels good," she muttered.

Yan Li hovered at his elbow. "Help?"

"Yes. When I lift her up, pull the blankets off the bed. Leave just the sheet."

Sam stepped in as Yan Li finished. "Maybe make soup?"

"No soup. Got any cold lemonade?"

The Chinese man grinned. "Make fast, Boss."

When he was alone with Winifred, he drew down the sheet and bathed the hot skin of her neck and chest, moved over her bare shoulders and down her arms, then her legs. If he weren't so worried about her, he'd stop to admire them—long and slim and well-shaped.

He dipped and sponged until Sam brought the lemonade and discreetly withdrew. Gently Zane helped Winifred sit up and pressed the glass to her lips. "Lemonade," he explained.

She drank greedily. "Good. More."

Oh, thank God, she could still swallow. He set the empty glass outside the door and went back to sponging her down.

"Zane," she whispered. "So hot."

He shoved up the window, praying for a cool breeze. No luck. The afternoon temperature had soared. He slammed it shut and loosened his shirt collar in the stifling air. Then he pulled the chair close to her bedside, rolled up his sleeves and set himself to saving Winifred's life.

At times Winifred opened her eyes and saw Zane's face above her, other times it was Yan Li or Sam who bent over her, soothing her sticky skin with cool water or helping her sip some refreshing liquid.

In her dreams she saw Papa, and then Mama, too, only she was young and Cissy was still in diapers. Orchestra conductors turned from their podiums to cue her; piano students played scales, over and over until she wanted to scream but found she could not make a sound. Then her father's nurse was speaking to her about Papa but she couldn't hear the words. The gardener brought bouquet after bouquet of yellow roses, and Papa's cook, the one he never liked, kept urging her to drink.

Her chest ached. Her head throbbed as if something heavy were smashing into her temples. Her eyelids burned underneath. Once she heard a man's voice and the word "hospital." Another man said "No."

And once a pair of tiny hands patted her arm and said her name, "'infred."

Oh, she wanted to wake up! Other times she wanted to sink into the soft blackness that settled around her.

On the day she finally opened her eyes, Zane stood over her, his stethoscope in his ears, the cool metal part pressed against the center of her chest.

He glanced into her face. "You're better," he said.

"How long have I been here?"

"Four days. And nights." His voice sounded grainy, as if he hadn't spoken for years and years.

"How did I get here? I remember boarding the train, but I don't remember getting off."

"You did. You were very sick, Winifred. And you're going to feel weak for some time."

"When is the wedding?"

He frowned down at her. "What wedding?"

"You know, Sarah Rose and Rooney…"

"Ah, I remember now. The twenty-ninth."

"What day is today?"

Zane's frown deepened. "Hell, I don't know. You arrived on the seventeenth… I'd say maybe it's the twenty-first?"

"I will be better by then, won't I?"

"Better, yes. Strong, no. We'll see about attending the wedding."

She laughed. "You sound like my doctor at home."

"I am your doctor, Winifred. And right now *this* is your home."

Men were so strange at times, she thought. Zane wasn't anything like Dr. Marcus in St. Louis. Zane was much more…well, outspoken. Pushy, even. He had undressed her, she realized, right down to her corset and chemise. Dr. Marcus would never…but of course she didn't have pneumonia then.

Or did she? She'd caught a chill two days before she left, but the doctor had never listened to her chest through a stethoscope.

"You are a wonderful doctor, Zane."

He laughed. "Not so wonderful. I spent a good many hours on my knees, asking God for help."

"You are wonderful," she contradicted. "Everyone says so. Even me."

"Were you sick before you left St. Louis?"

"Probably. I had a chill. I'd gone on a picnic, down by the river, the day before."

"A picnic? Who with?"

"With Dr. Beher. A professor from the conservatory. He teaches bassoon."

Zane just looked at her. "Bassoon," he echoed. "Not very romantic."

"Oh, no. Herman and I are just friends."

Zane's frown was back. After a long minute, during which he paced to and from the door, he asked, "Are you hungry? Yan Li made those little pancakes you like for breakfast."

"Is it breakfast time?" The sky outside her window was very blue, the sun well up.

"It isn't, no. But they warm up nicely. I'll just ask—"

"I must get up, Zane." She sat upright and tried to swing her legs over the edge of the bed, then realized she was naked under the sheet. "Oh! Where is my night robe?"

"You don't need it. You're not going downstairs."

Winifred just looked at the man. His expression was implacable. She'd seen it before, but it still surprised her how determined he could look. Like a bad-tempered watchdog.

"Besides," he added with a chuckle, "at the moment the cat is sleeping on your gown."

She followed his gaze to the chair, where the white cat was curled up on top of the blue silk.

"And besides that," he continued, his voice stern but his gray eyes twinkling, "you couldn't walk that far even if the house caught fire."

Oh, she couldn't? *Well, Dr. Dougherty, just you wait and see.*

## Chapter Eleven

It was two whole days before Winifred could talk Zane into letting her come downstairs for breakfast. But he'd been at the hospital most of the night, Sam told her. That, she thought, was just as well. He would never have agreed to her breakfast venture, but she was so weary of lying in bed and staring out the window at the blue summer sky she couldn't stand it one more minute.

She was unprepared for the effort it took to draw on her camisole and petticoat. Good heavens, she felt as weak as Sam's kitten. Just bending to lace up her shoes left her gasping for breath, and as for her corset, well, she just couldn't.

But she was determined to test her strength. She wanted in the worst way to attend Sarah and Rooney's wedding, and that was less than a week away. She dressed carefully in a pale blue dimity skirt and a short-sleeved white lawn waist.

She came down the stairs holding tight to the banister and placing her feet carefully on each step. Before she was halfway down, she felt light-headed. She seated herself at the dining room table, admiring the poached egg on toast Yan Li had made for her and listening to Rosemarie's baby talk as she petted the almost full-grown cat.

With a conspiratorial twinkle in his black eyes, Sam poured Winifred's coffee. How good it smelled! She hadn't been allowed anything stronger than tea for days and days.

After breakfast she watched her niece toddle unsteadily about the kitchen and the dining room. Yan Li dogged her steps but wisely let her try to walk. Most entertaining was the child's prattle. She caught "'infred" a number of times, and "'at," which she supposed meant "cat." The stream of unintelligible syllables flowed on, ending with "Yee" for Yan Li.

Winifred finished her coffee and rose to move into the library, but Rosemarie grabbed onto her skirt and tugged.

She bent down to pick her up but found she hadn't the strength to lift her. Oh, what now? She wanted to weep with frustration.

Instead, she took the girl's tiny hand in her own.

"Come with me, little one. Let's go into the library, shall we?" She matched her steps to Rosemarie's small ones and together they got as far as the doorway before Winifred had to stop and rest. My heavens, was she not strong enough to walk from one room to another?

Suppressing her annoyance, she knelt on the floor and invited Rosemarie into her arms. How warm and sweet-smelling she was! And she never stopped her happy chatter. Yan Li came to offer a pretty rag doll with a red gingham dress and Rosemarie scrambled out of Winifred's arms to grab for it.

"I watch," the Chinese girl said. "You rest?"

Yes. Winifred realized suddenly how short of breath she was. She rose, then had to grab for Yan Li's arm to steady herself. Her legs had turned to mush.

"I think I will go upstairs and lie down for a few minutes." Yan Li nodded and crouched beside Rosemarie to offer the doll again.

Winifred made it as far as the staircase, but then her legs began to shake. She felt dizzy and suddenly had to grab onto the banister. She leaned over the polished wood and tried to catch her breath and heard the front door open behind her.

"Winifred! What the hell…" Then Zane's strong hands were at her waist.

"I—I got tired all of a sudden."

"That's not surprising," he said, his voice stern. "You're not ready to get up."

"Yes," she interrupted. "I am ready. I just need a little time to—"

"You most certainly are not ready. I can see you're going to be a difficult patient."

She sucked in a breath. "And I can see you are going to be a difficult doctor."

He laughed at that. "I am, yes."

"Oh, Zane, let me try. I'm so tired of being sick." She straightened and set her foot on the first stair step. She tried, she really tried to heave her body up just that one four-inch step, but she couldn't manage it. Once again she leaned against the banister, gasping for air.

"That's it," Zane snapped. He hauled her up into his arms and strode up the stairs.

"Whoever thought climbing a single step would be so tiring?" she said against his neck.

He elbowed her door open. "Your doctor," he said shortly. "Who's seen enough pneumonia patients to know."

He laid her on the still unmade bed. "Now, close your eyes and think restful thoughts."

"Did anyone ever tell you that you are bossy as an old-maid schoolteacher?"

"Many times. I'm going to remove your shoes. And," he said after an awkward pause, "your skirt and your—"

"You will do no such thing!"

He laughed again. "It's a bit late for maidenly modesty, Winifred. After all, I've taken off your—"

"Don't say it." She rose up on one elbow. "It's positively scandalous to think that…" Her voice trailed off.

Zane pressed her back down onto the pillow. "Winifred, listen to me. I'm a doctor. I've seen hundreds of women unclothed."

"Yes, but did *you* unclothe them?"

He chuckled low in his throat. "Some, yes."

"How did you ever face them afterwards?"

"Like I'm facing you," he answered. "Good God, don't you remember that night you were so sick? No, apparently not. Winifred, sometimes you're more of a child than Celeste ever was."

"A child?" Now she was not just embarrassed, she was outraged. "*A child*?"

"I meant to say virginal," he amended.

Instantly she was up on her elbow again. "How do you know I am a—" She clapped her hand over her mouth and Zane smothered a grin.

"You mean," he said, his voice warmer than he might have liked, "your Professor—what was his name? Bassoon? That you and he, picnicking by the river on a warm summer afternoon, did not—?"

"Most certainly not," she snapped. "Herman Beher and I are just friends."

Zane laid his hand on her forehead to check for fever. "You and I are 'just friends,' Winifred. That doesn't preclude—I mean…"

She gazed up at him, her blue-green eyes widening. "Doesn't preclude what?"

"You have no fever," he said flatly.

"Doesn't preclude what?" she pursued. She waited, unblinking, for an answer.

Winifred, Zane acknowledged with an uncomfortable tightness in his chest, was as unlike Celeste as kittens were from cheetahs. Cheetahs chased their prey until it dropped.

"Doesn't preclude what?" she asked again.

Oh, for heaven's sake. "Doesn't preclude desire."

"Desire," she said, her voice tentative, as if weighing the word.

"Sexual desire, dammit." There, he'd said it. It had been on his mind for months; it was a relief to finally get it off his chest.

"Oh."

There was a long, pregnant silence. Zane's body heated in a long, slow dance he hadn't felt since… since his marriage. He couldn't think of a single thing to say.

"Oh," she said again.

Zane gave himself a mental jab in the ribs. "You

are not to get out of bed again until I say so, understood?"

"I think—I think I am...flattered."

He blinked. Her remark was irrelevant. Well, perhaps not so irrelevant, considering where the previous conversation had strayed. And then his mind jerked back to the matter underlying everything.

"Flattered," she breathed again.

"*Flattered*?" Hell.

"Yes, flattered."

There was a stunned silence.

"Zane, you look just like Papa used to when I shocked him."

"Did you shock him often?"

She looked up at him, her eyes amused, a little smile playing around her mouth. "As often as I possibly could."

Zane dragged in a long breath, then blew out a sigh. "You must have been a difficult girl to raise. A trial, in fact. I feel a great deal of sympathy for your father."

Winifred laughed softly. "Papa adored me. And I adored him, even though I was away at school for months at a time. But he did love me, and that helped."

Zane studied her. He could believe "difficult." And he could most definitely believe "adored."

She laid one arm over her eyes. "Were we finished?"

"We were, yes."

Well, no, they weren't, in fact. But Winifred was still too weak from her illness to take things any further. In fact, at this moment, he himself was feeling somewhat weak. He fought an urge to mop his forehead with his handkerchief.

"Get some rest," he ordered. He backed out of her bedroom and headed down the stairs, straight for the brandy decanter.

For the next few days, Winifred rose each morning, dressed and waited until she was sure Zane had left the house. When she heard the front door close, she carefully made her way downstairs to breakfast, played peekaboo with Rosemarie and tried a few passages on the piano just to keep her memory sharp. She had a concert early in September.

Then she climbed slowly back up the stairs to lie down, acknowledging that Zane was right about demanding that she rest. She would need all her strength when she returned to the conservatory for the fall term.

In the afternoon Sam or Yan Li would bring up tea and later would wake her for supper. But this afternoon was so clear and beautiful outside, and she felt so much stronger she decided to take a book of Milton's poetry out to the front porch and rock in the lawn swing while she read.

She had just stepped into the entry hall when the front door opened abruptly and a face wreathed in blond ringlets poked into the hall.

"Oh!" the young woman said, her cheeks turning pink. "What are *you* doing here?"

Winifred's hands clenched as she opened her mouth. "A better question, Mrs. Bledsoe, is what are *you* doing here? Do you make a habit of entering private homes without first ringing the bell?"

Darla Bledsoe stared at her. "I thought you lived in St. Louis?"

"I do live in St. Louis. I am a guest here."

"But why?" Darla's eyes narrowed into two hard stones.

"I came to visit my niece, my sister's child."

But Darla's question whirled around and around in Winifred's brain. She had to think about that. Yes, why *was* she here?

She felt she owed it to Cissy to be a presence in Rosemarie's life, but it was more than that. She had fallen in love with her sister's baby girl at first glance. She was so beautiful, so tiny and perfect, her fingers delicate and her eyes…oh, her eyes were that same blue-green Cissy's eyes had been.

Her breath stopped. Rosemarie filled an aching hollow in her own life.

Good heavens, that could not possibly be true. Her life in St. Louis was crammed full of everything she loved, her music, her students, her colleagues at the conservatory. She was sought after for piano performances, and she had her teaching, endless preparation for concerts and recitals, faculty conferences, even an occasional picnic or opera with a fellow professor. And before Papa died, she'd had him to love and care for.

Was that not enough?

Of course it was enough. Her existence was dizzyingly busy. In fact, the pace had been so frantic these past months she had felt continually exhausted. So exhausted, she admitted, that she had fallen ill with pneumonia and was now struggling to regain her strength. Zane said even now she was still "run-down."

Darla was saying something, but Winifred couldn't focus on the words. "I beg your pardon?"

"I said," the young woman enunciated carefully, her tone sharp, "doesn't a famous pianist have enough to keep her busy in St. Louis?"

Winifred blanched at Darla's rudeness and simply stared at her, unable to speak. No, it was not enough. It had never occurred to her before, but it *wasn't* enough.

*But why isn't it?*

Darla advanced another step into the entry hall and Winifred jerked to attention. "Dr. Dougherty is at the hospital all afternoon."

"No, I am not," a male voice from the porch steps interjected.

Darla pivoted, her stylish muslin skirt belling about her feet. "Zane!"

"Good afternoon, Darla. Do you need an appointment?"

"What? Oh, no, I am quite well. I just dropped by to…" Her gaze settled on Winifred.

Winifred knew the young woman wanted her to leave her alone with Zane, but something inside her refused to retreat a single step. Zane stepped up onto the porch. Darla was blocking the doorway, but she didn't move. A standoff, Winifred thought. If they had pistols, it might be a shoot-out.

Finally Zane took Darla's arm and pulled her out of the doorway. "Is there something I can do for you?" Adroitly he stepped around her.

"Yes, there is. I came by to invite you to a whist party at my house this evening."

"Sorry, I don't play whist."

"I could teach—"

Zane plunked his leather medical bag down on the hall floor. "I'm afraid I'll be at the hospital this evening."

Darla's lower lip pushed into a pout. "You're always at the hospital. Every party I give, you're busy at that old hospital."

"I'm a doctor, Darla. I work at 'that old hospital.' I have patients who are dying, patients getting born. What makes you think whist is more important than that?"

Winifred turned away and discreetly retreated into the dining room where both Sam and Yan Li instantly busied themselves with setting out plates for supper. She didn't dare look at either one.

"Lady chase Boss," Sam whispered. Yan Li poked her elbow into his ribs and he ducked his head.

"Yes," Winifred said quietly. "I see that." No doubt everyone in Smoke River saw it as well. Was that how women ended up marrying a man, by pursuing him until he gave up?

Cissy had not done that; Zane had pursued her sister, not the other way around.

She shrugged and met Sam's eye. It was no concern of hers.

*But you don't want Darla to trap Zane, do you?*

No, she admitted. She didn't want anyone to trap him.

Oh, what nonsense! *Why should I care?*

Yan Li again poked her husband in the ribs, then dropped her head to hide her expression.

Of course she shouldn't care!

But she did.

Oh, for mercy's sake, her thoughts were tumbling like dry leaves in a stiff breeze. She must still be feverish.

She retreated to her bedroom with the volume of Milton's poems and read until she fell asleep with the book open on her chest.

When she woke the sun outside the window painted the hills a soft gold and someone was tapping at her door.

"You want tea, missy?" Yan Li's soft voice brought her fully awake.

"Yes, thank you, Yan Li. I'll come downstairs. Where is Rosemarie?"

"In piano room with Mister. Bring tea there."

Winifred patted her disheveled chignon into a semblance of respectability, smoothed down her skirt and descended the stairs. Not a sound came from the "piano room." Usually Rosemarie gurgled and crowed her incomprehensible little words with such volume you could hear her all over the house; but not today, it seemed.

She stepped into the library and stopped short. Zane lay stretched out on the carpet, his baby daughter clasped belly-down against his chest. Both were sound asleep.

Winifred's heart gave a queer little thump. She

tiptoed in and settled herself in her favorite green velvet wingback chair and opened the Milton. Seven poems later, Zane's voice startled her.

"What are you reading?"

"Milton," she whispered, afraid to wake Rosemarie.

"Ah." One hand caressed his daughter's back. "Sabrina fair," he recited. "Listen where you are sitting, in twisted braids of lilies knitting—" He broke off as the baby stirred.

"Do you like poetry, Zane?" It had never occurred to her that any physician would have an education other than medicine. But then Zane wasn't just "any physician."

"I like Milton," he answered. "And Tennyson, and—"

Rosemarie woke up, immediately scrambled off Zane's chest and launched herself at Winifred's knees.

"Well, hello, little one. Did you have a nice nap with your papa?"

"'Infred," the child announced. She tugged at Winifred's blue dimity skirt and raised both arms to be picked up.

She lifted the child onto her lap, noting that she wore the ruffled pink dress she had sent at Christmas. "Shall I read you a story?"

The child snuggled against her bosom and

began playing with the mother-of-pearl buttons on her blue-striped shirtwaist. Winifred picked up her book, paged to the middle and spread it open as if finding a story.

"Once upon a time," she began. "In a land far, far away, there lived a—"

Yan Li entered with the tea tray, set it down on the small oak table at Winifred's side and handed Rosemarie a cookie.

"'ookie," the baby squealed, crumbling it in her small fist.

Yan Li bent to hand Zane a cup and saucer, which he absently set on the floor beside him. He wasn't looking at his tea; he was looking at Winifred.

"Go on," he said. "I want to hear the story."

She swallowed back a burble of laughter. "It isn't about Sabrina," she cautioned.

He grinned. "Make it about you," he suggested.

"Me! No child wants to hear a story about the storyteller."

"I do," he said quietly. "Go on, I'm waiting."

Yan Li laughed softly and offered to take the baby, but Winifred shook her head. Rosemarie sat perfectly still while cookie crumbs rained onto Winifred's skirt. She pointed her sticky forefinger at the open page.

"Very well. Once upon a time there lived a little girl who loved to eat cookies."

"Did you?" Zane broke in.

"Well, yes, I did as a matter of fact. Chocolate ones in particular. I left my handprints on every piece of furniture in the house and most of the curtains."

"And then what?"

"Why, I grew up, of course. Zane, one day you will look back on afternoons like this with Rosemarie and cookies and tea and it will make you…" She caught a flicker of something in his gaze that stopped her breath. Pain, mixed with a hungry longing. "…it will make you glad."

Zane laid his arm over his eyes. "Is there more to the story?"

Winifred caught Rosemarie's waving, crumb-coated hand in her own. "No. There is no more to the story. The girl grew up and attended conservatory with her sister and embarked on a career as a pianist. And that is the end."

"But it's not the end," he said. "It has not been enough, has it? That was why you wanted to raise Celeste's child, was it not? You want to give your own life meaning beyond what you have clung to all these years."

"No, Zane. You are quite wrong. I felt that I owed Cissy…"

Slowly he sat up and looked at her. Something zinged between them and she couldn't look away from his accusing gray eyes. Suddenly she found herself wondering all sorts of things, about him. About Cissy.

About herself.

"Winifred," he said, his voice quiet. "Would you care to play some whist this evening after supper?"

"But you don't play whist. I heard you tell Darla this morning…"

He held her gaze and a smile tugged at his mouth. "I do play whist. Just not with Darla."

She nodded but could not think of a thing to say. They drank their tea in silence, Zane cross-legged on the floor and Winifred in the chair with Rosemarie on her lap until she began to fuss.

"Not another tooth, I hope," Winifred said.

"More likely she wants another cookie. Or," he said with a low chuckle, "maybe she feels left out and wants to play whist, too."

## Chapter Twelve

They played whist until almost midnight, when the clang of the doorbell startled them. Zane heaved himself out of his chair and went into the hall to answer it, returning within minutes. "I've got to go out. Ellie Johnson is in labor."

"The schoolteacher?"

"Maybe, maybe not. Married women aren't usually allowed to teach school in Oregon. They made an exception for Ellie when she became pregnant. Matt, her husband, wants her to continue, but even a federal marshal can't order the school board around."

Winifred began gathering up the playing cards.

"Maybe it's just as well," he said. "I haven't lost this many hands playing cards since my medical school days."

"I'll wait up for you and make some coffee."

"Don't. Might be gone all night and tomorrow, too."

"Is Mrs. Johnson at the hospital? I could bring—"

"Nope. I'll take a horse and ride out to their place. Go to bed, Winifred. Get some rest. Tomorrow is Rooney and Sarah's wedding. Four o'clock at Rose Cottage. I'll try to be there."

She watched him step into his office for his black leather medical bag, then heard him move through the kitchen and out the back door to the barn. No sooner had the door closed than Sam appeared.

"Boss go out?"

"Yes. A baby is on the way."

"Work too hard," the houseboy observed.

"A physician has no choice, Sam. Medicine is his chosen calling." *Just as music is mine. But I do have a choice. I haven't sworn a sacred oath, as Zane has.*

She packed the deck of cards into the walnut holder and stashed it on the bookshelf between Wordsworth and Sir Walter Scott. Sam disappeared into the kitchen and, she supposed, back to bed with Yan Li. How wonderful it must be to have each other, to talk to each other every day and be with each other every night for the rest of their lives.

Upstairs, she undressed and crawled into bed to

find her cheeks wet. Just fatigue, she told herself. Fatigue and…and what? Well, she had been quite sick with pneumonia; perhaps she was not yet fully recovered. Perhaps her nerves had been affected by her illness. Or perhaps winning so many hands of whist had tired out her mind.

Still, the last time she had wept was at Papa's funeral, when she had felt overwhelming emptiness, the aching loss of someone she loved. And she had felt so terrible, so guilty, when she couldn't be at Cissy's funeral. She lay down on her narrow bed and swiped her hand across her eyes.

At a quarter to four the following afternoon, Zane had not returned. Winifred walked down the hill to Rose Cottage for the wedding of Sarah Rose and Rooney Cloudman, sending a silent prayer for Ellie Johnson's safe delivery. Sam had unearthed a blue lace-trimmed parasol of Cissy's, for which she was grateful; the sun was scorching.

On the front porch of the boardinghouse, which Sarah ran, Winifred folded the parasol, then walked through the wide open front doorway and gasped. Huge bouquets of roses, crimson, yellow, even lavender, sat on every available table and swathed the fireplace mantel. Smaller vases of orange zinnias and black-eyed Susans decorated the dining table in the next room, surrounding a spectacular many-layered wedding cake. Oh, it was so beautiful she wanted to cry.

Dr. Samuel Graham, Zane's partner, greeted the arriving guests. "Zane isn't back yet, I gather?" the graying physician asked.

"Not yet. I hope everything is all right."

"It will be. I've never known Zane to lose a mother, except for—" He snapped his mouth shut and took her hand. "I beg your pardon, Miss Von Dannen. I recall now that Celeste was your sister."

Winifred nodded and moved on into the parlor. Jeanne and Wash Halliday were there with their young daughter, Manette. Winifred guessed this was the girl who had fallen out of the tree some months before. Leah MacAllister stood with them.

How lovely she was, with her almond-shaped gray eyes and alabaster skin. And such cheekbones! Her husband, Thad, was deep in conversation with the groom, Rooney Cloudman, who looked rigid as a department store floorwalker in his dark suit and tie.

Rooney looked up and started across the room toward her. "Glad yer here, Miss Winifred. Thought ya could give me some advice about my nerves. Stage fright, I guess you'd call it."

She grasped the hands he extended toward her. "Why, Rooney, you're not nervous, are you?"

"Never been so scared in all my life, not even

fightin' Indians with Wash Halliday. Never been really married, ya see. My first wife was Cherokee. Indians don't go through all this…" He gestured to the milling townspeople in the room. "Fol-de-rol, I guess you'd call it."

"Don't think about the crowd, Rooney. Just take a deep breath and keep breathing in and out, nice and slow. Think about Sarah."

"Hell's bells, Miss Winifred, that's what got me so scared. I'd do most anything for Sarah and I surely want her to be happy. With me, I mean. I mean married to me." He wiped his tanned face with the handkerchief he snatched from his breast pocket.

Winifred patted his arm and smiled at him. "She will be happy with you, Rooney. I know she will."

With a grateful look, he moved off.

Reverend Pollock, his cherubic countenance beaming, made his way to the front of the room and tapped on the mantelpiece for attention. When the crowd quieted, Sarah Rose descended the staircase wearing a lovely lavender dimity afternoon dress and carrying a bouquet of dark purple clematis. Even from where she was standing, Winifred could see Sarah's hands shake. The crowd parted for her and she heard Rooney suck in his breath.

Sarah looked up at him and when he stepped

to her side, Winifred's heart kicked. The woman's happiness was luminous.

Sarah's grandson, Mark, took his place beside her and Wash Halliday stepped up to stand with Rooney. Sarah handed her flowers to Mark and clasped Rooney's offered hand.

"*Dearly beloved…*"

In the next instant Zane was beside her, breathing hard as if he'd been running. "Girl," he murmured in her ear.

"*…this man and this woman…*"

He stood close enough that she could feel the heat from his body and catch a whiff of his spicy shaving lotion. Surreptitiously he took her hand, brushing their entwined fingers against his light flannel-covered thigh.

"*…to have and to hold from this day forth…*"

Zane moved his shoulder to touch hers and stood gazing straight ahead at the couple as they exchanged their vows.

Winifred's breath grew ragged. She was going to cry. Was crying. Oh, dear God, this was so beautiful.

Zane pressed her fingers.

"*You may kiss the bride.*"

She couldn't watch. It seemed so private, joining one's life with another. Instead, she dropped her gaze to the floor and felt Zane's hand squeeze hers again. He understood. Of course he did. He knew what it was to love someone, to pledge to honor and cherish her. He knew because he had loved Cissy.

Ever since her sister's death she had felt envious of what Cissy had had with this man. Perhaps she, too, would have done what Cissy had; set aside everything to be with Zane. She had never really understood it before, but she did now, at this moment.

Zane offered his handkerchief. She snatched it, feeling more unstrung than she ever had in recitals or concerts, even when she was just starting out on her performing career. She mopped at her welling eyes and tried to control her breathing.

The room erupted in cheers and began moving into the dining room for refreshments. Zane steered her in the opposite direction, out onto the honeysuckle-draped front porch.

She couldn't seem to stop crying. Zane settled her into the porch swing. "Gets to you, doesn't it?"

"Y-yes, it does. I think I will never attend another wedding after this."

He gave her a long, unsmiling look. "I'll bring us some cake and lemonade."

While he was gone, Winifred tried to calm herself down. Goodness, her nerves were disintegrating! She hoped someone would add some hard cider to the lemonade.

Zane stepped out the front door, one hand balancing two plates of wedding cake and the other clutching two tall glasses of lemonade. Two forks stuck out of his jacket pocket.

Winifred took one look at him and again burst into tears.

"I don't know what's the matter with me," she sobbed.

"I do. You've kept yourself away from things like this, away from life."

"No, I haven't. My life is very full. I'm so busy with my music, with teaching and performing, I can scarcely keep up."

He thrust a glass of lemonade into her hands. "Take a big swallow, Winifred. Now take a deep breath."

A choked laugh escaped her. "That's exactly what I told Rooney before the ceremony, for his nerves. I suppose wedding jitters are l-like stage fright."

Zane set a white china plate of wedding cake in her lap and pulled a fork out of his pocket. "Want to hear about Ellie Johnson's baby?"

She nodded and stabbed at her cake.

"Beautiful baby girl. Lots of dark hair. Big blue eyes. Matt has fallen in love all over again."

She sniffled. "I felt just like that when I first saw Rosemarie."

"Ellie and Matt's wedding was a bit unusual," he said after a moment of silence. "Matt got tired of waiting while the flower girl and all the bridesmaids sashayed down the aisle, so he charged down, picked Ellie up and carried her up to the altar himself. People talked about it for weeks."

Winifred laughed. "No stage fright, I guess."

"None," Zane agreed. He studied the plate before him. "Good cake."

Suddenly she realized he had successfully gotten her to stop crying. "You're a good doctor, Zane."

"Not very good at whist, though."

"Maybe not, but you're good with hysterical females, good with pneumonia cases, good with mothers having bab—" *Except for Cissy.*

She closed her eyes in anguish. "Oh, Zane, I'm sorry. I'm so sorry."

He said nothing, just forked bites of cake into his mouth and washed them down with lemonade. When his plate was clean, he set it on the floor of the porch and turned toward her.

"I am good with women having babies, Winifred. Celeste didn't die in childbirth. But she hemorrhaged afterward, and I couldn't stop it. I have never felt so helpless in my life."

"Oh, Zane. I—"

"Now, let's go inside and congratulate Mr. and Mrs. Cloudman." He took her plate and the empty lemonade glass, set them on the floor and stood up. "Damn, I could sure use a shot of whiskey."

"Oh, so could I!"

They walked home slowly in the cooling dusk, the air soft and scented with roses and honeysuckle, the evening song sparrows audible over the neighborhood sounds of children's hopscotch and piano practice.

"Do you like Smoke River?" Zane asked suddenly.

"Yes, I do. It's a pretty town. The people are friendly."

"Do you think—?"

"No," she said quickly. "I don't."

Zane lifted his eyebrows at her over-fast response, but he didn't argue or challenge. He merely took her hand and kept on walking.

## Chapter Thirteen

Winifred tossed the sheet off her sticky body and sat upright. She couldn't sleep. It was too hot, and the July air outside her wide open window smelled so sweet and delicious it made her ache. Why, *why* did everyone in Smoke River have to grow roses or jasmine or honeysuckle or other things that smelled so evocative?

What was wrong with her?

All at once she heard Cissy's voice. *Nothing is wrong, you silly. You're just alive.*

She felt as jumpy as Sam's cat. Restless and short-tempered. At supper she'd snapped at Zane about everything, the soup, the mint tea Sam had brewed for her, even the salt and pepper shakers they passed back and forth. Every time their fingers brushed she wanted to scream. Or cry. Or both.

After supper Zane had made fresh peach ice cream, refusing to let Sam or Yan Li take over turning the crank and refusing to believe her when she said she didn't want any. He simply chuckled in that maddening way of his, scooped up a big dish and plunked it in her lap. Then, when she'd absentmindedly eaten it all up, he laughed.

Oh, why did this man make her so mad?

She slipped out of bed and padded to the open window. The moon was up, spilling silvery light over the quiet street and the wide meadow beyond the house. It gilded the field of wild buckwheat stalks and the low-growing blue daisy-like flowers so they looked like miniature swords and tiny shields. It was beautiful out there, so serene and untroubled it looked like a Monet painting.

She should read something until she grew sleepy. But lately even Milton was making her cry. *Everything* made her cry.

She could write to Millicent in St. Louis... No, she'd be vacationing at her home in Rochester. Millicent had wanted her to come home with her for the summer, but Winifred could hardly wait to come west to see Rosemarie. And Zane.

She could steal silently downstairs and out onto the porch.

Maybe rocking in the swing would settle her nerves.

And maybe not. The sound of crickets made her jumpy, reminded her of creatures that made noise to attract mates—bullfrogs and nightingales and owls. Did owls mate at night? What about swans? And wolves and…and giraffes? How annoying. Why did all God's creatures have to mate?

She drew in an uneven breath. Because if they did not, the creatures of the earth would die off and life would cease. The cycle of birth and death would stop and Milton's paradise would be truly lost.

She didn't know how long she stood staring out at the moon-bathed grass and silver-leafed trees, but it didn't help her jangled nerves or her fluttery heart one bit. Instinctively she knew that nothing would help; she would have to unjangle her own nerves, as she did on performance nights. But, she wondered, how did one unflutter one's heart?

The next morning promised to be another scorching day, and by ten o'clock Winifred had exhausted a lemon meringue pie lesson, Milton and a frustrating practice session on her Mozart piano concerto.

Rosemarie was always quiet when she played the piano; the baby sat motionless in the makeshift playpen Sam had rigged up out of apple crates, apparently listening; the minute Winifred stopped to mark something on the score, Rosemarie set up a wail of protest.

Another year and her niece could reach the piano keys, and then the household would never be the same. Maybe when Rosemarie was older, Winifred could start teaching her the rudiments of beginning piano.

Maybe. Winifred wasn't sure she could stand another summer out here in Smoke River. She always returned to St. Louis and the conservatory so unsettled it took days to focus on the curriculum and her students.

This morning Zane had patients to see. Now he emerged from his office surgery looking hot and tired, tossed his flannel jacket onto a library chair and pulled off his tie. Winifred stopped playing and swiveled toward him; her hands were perspiring so much her fingers were slipping off the keys.

"Hot," he said.

"Too hot," she responded. Suddenly she scooted off the piano bench. "Zane, could we go swimming?"

He looked at her oddly and didn't answer.

"Please? Could we? It's so hot today."

Zane glanced to the playpen where Rosemarie sat poking the remains of a soggy cookie into her mouth. It was time for her nap. True, today was much hotter than yesterday, but swimming with Winifred?

He frowned and shook his head. Not a good idea, no matter how hot it was.

Winifred came toward him, her eyes alight. "Please say yes, Zane. *Please.*"

Good God almighty, he couldn't refuse her anything. He nodded shortly. "I'll get Sam to make up a picnic bask—"

She didn't hear the rest; she'd flown up the staircase with more energy than he'd seen in a week.

"You're not to swim, Winifred," he ordered when she returned. "You understand? You've had pneumonia, and you can't risk getting chilled. It'll still be cooler for you in the shade around the hole, though."

She looked so disappointed that a dart of guilt laced into him, but as a physician he knew he was right to insist.

With a sigh she deposited a bundle he supposed was a bathing costume on the library chair.

She sat beside him on the buggy seat, shaded with that lacy-looking parasol, and sighed dramatically. "Swimming would cool me off," she said.

"Don't whine. I'm your doctor, remember?"

Her shoulders drooped. "Oh, all right. I'll sit in

the shade and…think. Or do something equally unathletic."

He clicked his tongue at the horse and rolled off the dusty town road onto the narrow lane that led to the swimming hole. Good. He wouldn't have to look at her lush body in a swimming suit. Covered up from her ankles to her neck, as she was now in the yellow-striped skirt and shirtwaist, he should be perfectly safe.

But as soon as she climbed down and fluffed out her skirt, he glimpsed her ruffled petticoat and knew he was wrong. He would never feel safe around Winifred. He was always going to notice her, feel her eyes regarding him with interest or amusement or pique or with overflowing tears.

He knew now what he'd been denying for months; he was always going to notice Winifred Von Dannen.

And he was always going to want her.

It wasn't the same kind of wanting he'd known with Celeste, the heady, star-spangled rush of blind desire. He let out a groan. This wasn't the same at all.

Winifred stopped en route to the shady spot between two vine maples and turned toward him. "What is wrong?"

"Nothing," he said quickly. "Just tired, I guess. Too many patients this morning."

"Darla Bledsoe?" Her eyes sparkled with one of those looks she got when something tickled her. "Another broken ...toe, was it?"

"This time it was a sprained finger," he said dryly. "Lifting a heavy washtub."

Winifred laughed and sat down in the shade, settling her skirt around her. "You know, Zane, by the time Darla finally hog-ties you, she won't be able to—"

Her cheeks turned crimson.

Zane laughed and dropped down beside her with the picnic basket. "Oh, yes, she will. Darla is not easily deterred."

She gave him a thoughtful look. "Do you want to deter Darla? Really?"

"Dammit, Winifred. How can you ask that?"

She blanched and he was instantly sorry. Oh, hell. He couldn't sit here beside her, smelling her hair, feeling the warmth of her body for one more minute.

"I'm going swimming," he announced. He stood, stripped off his chambray shirt and shucked his denims down to his drawers while her eyes rounded in shock. Then he sprinted for the water.

He swam twenty laps in the cold water, then ten more for good measure. When he emerged with his wet drawers leaving nothing to the imagination, he threw himself facedown beside her. "Good thing I'm not naked, Winifred, because you look like you've seen a ghost."

"Not a ghost," she said in a shaky voice. "Just a man with…with…"

He sat up, spraying water droplets onto her yellow blouse. "All men have them," he quipped. "I bet even Dr. Bassoon has—"

"Oh, no," she interrupted. "I mean, he has never—"

"Never undressed in front of you?" He rolled away from her stricken face.

"He has never gone swimming with me."

"*We* are not swimming," he said, trying not to laugh. "*I* am the one swimming. *You* are supposed to be resting."

Her breath hissed in. The long silence that followed made him uneasy. Then he heard a choked sound. "Just you wait and see," she murmured.

He heard the soft plop of her shoes dropping onto the sand, then a swish and out of the corner of his eye he caught a blur of white petticoat. No. She wouldn't dare.

He bolted upright.

Too late. Her clothes lay in a heap beside him and when he looked up there she was, striding away toward the river in nothing but her lace-trimmed drawers and camisole. Oh, hell. He should chase her down and tackle her before she reached the water. On second thought he should ready a towel and wait until she came out of the river and rub her down before she took a chill. Damn, what a choice.

She thrashed about in the chest-high water, upended her body so her rump poked up above the surface, and splashed happily in a big circle. Her hair came unpinned and floated about her shoulders. When she grew tired, she dog-paddled toward him.

As she emerged, her wet camisole stuck to her breasts and Zane caught his breath. He shouldn't look at her. But he couldn't *not* look at her.

Her drawers clung to her hips, revealing her clearly defined waist, the curve of her buttocks and—oh, God—the triangle of dark hair at the apex of her thighs.

He snatched up the larger of the two bath towels and advanced toward her with long strides. "Here." He wrapped her up tightly and immediately turned his back.

"Oh, that w-was just w-wonderful!" Her teeth were chattering and Zane swore again.

"Strip and dry off," he ordered.

"Y-yes. I am r-rather cold. But it w-was worth it."

"Was it?" he bit out. "You are the most foolhardy, most headstrong woman I've ever known." He kept talking with his back to her until he was sure she had disappeared behind a huckleberry bush. When he turned, he noticed her wet garments still lay on the ground beside him.

He also noticed that his entire frame was shaking.

Her voice came from behind the shrubbery. "Hand me my skirt and shirtwaist, would you, Zane? And my petticoat."

He balled them up and tossed them over the bush.

When she emerged, her smile sent an arrow of fire up his spine. Even clothed as she now was, he couldn't look at her. He knew damn well she had nothing on underneath.

He tried not to watch her as she settled beside him and grabbed her shoes and stockings. Then her hand stilled.

"You won't mind if I don't put my stockings back on, will you? I feel so...well, exposed."

He laughed. She eyed him slantwise and that just made it worse.

"Well," she huffed. "I'll just wring out my—"

"Don't," he managed to choke out. "I'll spread them out on the bushes and they'll be dry in ten minutes."

Another mistake. He picked up her soft lacy drawers and camisole and squeezed the water out, trying to keep himself from squashing them into his hands and burying his face in them to inhale her scent. With a cavalier gesture he flung each small piece of erotic temptation over the huckleberry bush. He found he was breathing much too hard.

When he returned to her side, she was digging in the wicker picnic basket. She looked up at him and smiled.

"Breast or thigh?"

"Winifred," he said in a strangled voice. He'd had all he could take. He dropped to her side, lifted the basket away and pulled her into his arms.

## Chapter Fourteen

Zane tipped her face up and covered her mouth with his. "Don't tease me like this, Winifred," he said against her lips. "You're not Darla Bledsoe."

She opened her eyes. "Does she tease you?"

He pressed his mouth to her forehead. "Not like this, dammit. Winifred, are you even aware of what you're doing?"

"No. Yes," she amended. "I didn't know this was teasing," she murmured.

"What the hell did you think it was?"

She didn't answer, just held on to him. He could feel her heart beating against his bare chest.

"What?" he repeated.

"I guess I just like getting under your skin, Zane," she said with a soft laugh. "You can be so bossy sometimes."

He resisted the urge to shake her until her teeth

rattled. "You're under my skin, all right. You're under my skin day and night, especially at night. I've started putting in more time at the hospital to get through your visits."

"Oh," she said in a small voice. "I didn't know."

He groaned. "How can you *not* know?"

"Well, yes, I did know," she admitted after a moment. "I just didn't want to think about it."

He said nothing. The scent of her hair was driving him crazy. She didn't move for a long time, and then she pulled away, gave him a wobbly smile, and met his gaze. Her eyes looked a little dazed.

"Are you hungry?"

He jerked. "What?"

"I mean, should we eat our lunch now?"

"No," he retorted sharply. "Yes. Don't ask any more suggestive questions like that."

"Very well," she breathed. "I promise." She didn't sound the least bit chastened, but she offered the picnic basket as if nothing was the least bit out of the ordinary.

Exasperated, he lifted it out of her hand, set it on the ground and forced her chin up to look straight into her eyes. "Winifred, I can't go on like this."

Her smile faded. "I am sorry, Zane. I don't know much…actually I don't know anything about… about…"

"About a man and a woman," he supplied. That much was obvious. From what Celeste had told him, neither of the Von Dannen sisters had had any experience with the opposite sex.

Especially not Winifred. *She was so dedicated,* Celeste had said. *She worked so hard and she never let herself have any fun.*

That explained why his wife had been stiff and frightened on their wedding night. And maybe it explained Winifred, too. While he knew Winifred liked him, it was clear she had no idea of his deepening feelings for her.

His breath stopped. If she did know, would she bolt?

He rocked her in his arms and tried to think. *Tell her.* No, he couldn't risk it.

*Maybe she has already guessed?* He didn't think so, at least after he'd kissed her at the train station at the end of her second visit, her attitude toward him hadn't seemed to change.

"Winifred, you know that I like you. I like you quite a bit, in fact."

"Yes," she said softly. "I know."

"Does it…offend you?"

"You mean because you are my brother-in-law? To be truthful, I no longer think of you that way. You kissed me after the Christmas dance, remember? You said it was premature. Not wise. But not wrong."

"And?" He held his breath waiting for her answer.

"And I believed you. It is not wrong for you to kiss me."

Zane gritted his teeth. "What about 'premature' and 'not wise'?"

"Well, yes, I think perhaps it is still not wise."

"Because of what people might say?" Again, he held his breath.

"Oh, heavens no. I've never paid any attention to what people think about what I do. Kissing me is not wise because you live here in Smoke River and I live in St. Louis.

"Your career as a physician is here. Mine is at the conservatory in the East."

"Oh," he said, his voice flat.

"I raise a lot of eyebrows in St. Louis because I have no wish to marry. Because I have dedicated my life to music, to my students and to performing as a pianist."

"Dammit, Winifred, you make it sound so logical, and it isn't."

She looked up and he saw tears shimmering on her lashes. "Zane, perhaps it is not logical, but that is the way it is. Still," she added, her voice throaty, "that does not mean…that I do not care for you. That I do not want, well, more."

He groaned. "What does that mean, 'more'?"

"Well…more. I like it when you talk to me. And I, um, I like it when you kiss me."

"Thank God," he murmured.

"Zane, I think we should finish our picnic and return to town."

That was the last thing he wanted to do, but he forced himself to drop his arms and get his breathing under control.

Later, when he had pulled on his trousers and shirt, Winifred set out the fried chicken and lemonade and napkins Sam had packed. Her fingers were shaking.

Zane found he couldn't take his eyes off her hands. And he couldn't stop smiling.

They drove back in the buggy to the road in a silence so complete Winifred fancied she could hear her heart beating. She did like Zane's kisses, more than Professor Beher's or even Pierre de Fulet's on the terrace after the reception following her Boston debut. Zane had kissed her before today; twice, in fact. Both times were startling, not because he had been Cissy's husband, but more because she liked him, liked feeling his lips touch hers. Last Christmas at the train station she had wanted to kiss him back, but the train was leaving and there was no time.

*And now?* Her pulse skipped. Today when he kissed her she'd wanted it to go on and on. When his mouth found hers she felt as if her skin would split wide open and she would fly away.

She watched his hands on the reins. His skin was tanned, his fingers long and capable-looking, skilled at probing with surgical instruments or smoothing witch hazel over a sunburn. She was in awe of this man. And she liked sitting close to him and not talking.

She edged toward him a few inches and laid her head against his shoulder. No one would see them; they had not yet reached the road back to town.

Zane made a sound in his throat, pulled the horse to a stop and wound the reins around the brake handle. He turned to her, his gray eyes dark and smoky. He caught her mouth under his, moving his lips over hers slowly, purposefully. She wanted it to go on forever.

He deepened the kiss and she opened her lips. He tasted of lemons and something sweet, and all at once she wanted to weep.

She touched his arms, felt the muscles bunch and tremble. She ached for something more, something…closer.

"Zane," she murmured against his mouth. "Touch me."

His hands at her back stilled, then he slowly moved his fingers to the top mother-of-pearl button of her shirtwaist. He slipped it free, then moved to the next. Her skin felt as if it were spangled with stars.

He spread her bodice and kissed her collarbone, pressed his mouth along her neck, her throat. Her breasts began to swell. Dear God, this was heaven.

She arched toward him, desperate to feel his hands on her skin. He stroked one finger over her nipple and she gasped. A tingly, hungry sensation shot straight to a place below her belly.

His breathing grew rough, and the sound flooded her with a sense of power. This was like nothing she'd ever experienced, not even during a piano concerto when she felt the orchestra soaring with her and she knew she held the audience in the palm of her hand. This was so strong and beautiful she wanted to scream.

He slipped her shirtwaist off her shoulders, bent his head and drew his tongue over her breast. Heat danced along her veins and up her spine. Her nipples throbbed. She felt as if a slow fire were melting her bones.

Suddenly she wanted to be naked, wanted to feel his hard body pressed against hers. She moaned, and he lifted his head and looked into her eyes.

"I thank God we are sitting up," he murmured.

Winifred laughed softly. "And on a hard buggy seat at that."

This time he laughed, then his smile faded. "I hear someone coming." He began to rebutton her shirtwaist, then freed the reins and flapped them at the horse. His hands shook.

When they reached the road back to town they met Teddy MacAllister and another boy on horseback, fishing rods clutched in their hands. Zane let them pass and turned to Winifred with a wistful smile. "They almost got a lesson in lovemaking," he quipped.

"Aren't they too young?"

Zane gave her a long look. "They're male, aren't they? Boys notice girls early. By the time they're my age, they don't care anymore."

"Zane, you cannot be serious."

He sucked in a long breath. "Of course I'm not serious. Look at you and me and what is happening between us."

Oh, my. Winifred knew her face was turning scarlet.

Sam met them at the door. "Boss needed at hospital, quick!"

Zane swung the picnic basket into Sam's arms and headed to his office for his medical bag. On his way back to the front door, he stopped Winifred in the hallway.

"Wait for me."

And then he was gone.

## Chapter Fifteen

Dr. Samuel Graham met Zane in the hospital entryway, his face haggard. "Thank God you're here. We've got one helluva problem."

Zane dropped his black leather bag on the floor and ran one hand through his unruly still-damp hair. "What's happened?"

"Cholera."

His heart sank. He could still taste Winifred's lips, her skin; the last place he wanted to spend the night was at the hospital.

"You've set up an isolation ward?"

"Yes. Ten beds and it's almost full."

"Identify the source?"

"Contaminated stream serving eight families between here and Gillette Springs."

"Okay. Let's go to work."

They labored through the night and well into the morning forcing saline solutions down throats and wrapping shuddering bodies in warm blankets. At four in the morning Zane insisted Samuel go home to rest. By noon, his nurse, Elvira Sorensen, pushed him out of the ward and pressed his medical bag into his hand.

"Go home, Zane. We can manage until Dr. Sam gets back."

He nodded. He was out on his feet, but he hated leaving when patients were so ill. At least they hadn't lost any.

"I'll be back at midnight. Send a note if you need me before then."

The house was quiet when Zane quietly entered the front door. But before he could drop his bag on his desk, the doorbell jangled.

"Sam," he called. "Send whoever it is down to the hospital. I've got to get some sleep."

His houseboy nodded, but before Zane reached the staircase he heard a shrill female voice. "I know he's here. I just saw him walk up the hill from the hospital."

"Doctor very tired, missy. Need sleep."

"I'll just be a minute, so don't try to stop me."

"But missy—"

Zane turned his weary body back toward his office and watched Darla Bledsoe push her pink muslin-clad frame past Sam.

"Zane! You're just the man I need to—"

"Good morning, Darla. Or is it afternoon? I've just spent all night at the hospital and I'm a bit fuzzy."

"It's lunchtime. I thought we might—"

"No."

"But—"

"I'm not interested."

"Well, supper, maybe? After you—"

"Not interested," he repeated.

"Zane," she wheedled. "Please. Don't you—?"

Purposefully he took her elbow and steered her toward the front door. "Darla, this house is not only my medical office, it is my private residence as well. I would appreciate your not coming here unless you need medical help."

When the door closed, Zane expelled an angry breath and turned to find Sam watching him, his arms folded over his midriff. "Good ridding," he said with a sniff.

"Riddance, you mean. Yes. In future, you have my permission to shut the door in Mrs. Bledsoe's face."

Sam grinned. "Happy to do, Boss."

"Now, where is Winifred?"

"With baby Rose in bedroom. Both take nap after lunch."

Zane nodded and started again for the stairs. "Wake me for supper, Sam."

"Will do, boss. Missy, too. Make special."

Zane sighed wearily. Special, huh? It would be special to sit at the table across from Winifred and just look at her.

Zane slept until Sam tapped on his bedroom door to announce supper, and then he sat at the dining table bouncing a spoon impatiently against the tablecloth until Winifred appeared with Rosemarie in her arms.

He took the baby from her and while Sam and Yan Li set out the supper plates and a platter of cold meat and cheese, he cuddled his daughter, letting her pat her small hands over his neck and chin and play with his unbuttoned shirt collar. She smelled faintly of Winifred's spicy lavender soap.

"You gave her a bath?"

"We took a bath together."

He wished he hadn't asked. The vision of Winifred naked in the bathtub set his senses humming.

Yan Li brought two salad plates loaded with sliced cucumbers and tomatoes and lifted Rosemarie out of his arms. "I feed baby now. You eat." The slim, dark-haired girl disappeared into the kitchen with Rosemarie balanced on her hip.

Winifred shook out her napkin and lifted her

salad fork. "Did I hear Darla Bledsoe's voice this afternoon when you came back from the hospital?"

"You did. Where were you?"

"Sitting on the top step of the stairs." She dropped her gaze. "Eavesdropping," she added.

"Then you already know what she wanted."

"Yes, I do. She wants you, Zane."

"I— Yes, she does."

Winifred looked straight into his eyes. "She's all wrong for you."

"I know. She's too self-centered to be a doctor's wife."

She glanced up, her face oddly strained. "At least she is not career-centered," she murmured.

"Maybe," he said, his voice matter-of-fact. He crunched up a crisp slice of cucumber. "Maybe not."

"Zane?"

"I heard you," he said. "It changes nothing."

Winifred continued to fork bites of tomato into her mouth. The silence stretched until he could hear Rosemarie's happy chatter and Yan Li's soft voice from the kitchen. He was truly blessed with his beautiful baby daughter and two loyal servants. Friends, really. And a growing medical practice. He had a good life in a town he loved.

But he wanted more. He wanted Winifred.

"Sam said something about an epidemic. Is it very bad?"

"Cholera. And yes, it's bad."

Sam stepped in to retrieve the salad plates. "Okay I go play fan-tan with Ming Cha tonight?"

"I'd rather you didn't, Sam. I'm sorry, but cholera is highly contagious."

Sam sent him a frightened look. "You mean, Yan Li can catch?"

"Yan Li can catch it if she drinks contaminated water or touches anything that is contaminated. Keep her inside and scrub any vegetables you buy at the market. And boil all the water you drink."

"All from own garden," Sam said happily. "Yan Li grow."

"Eggs?"

"We have many chickens, Boss. And even milk cow."

Zane relaxed somewhat. Those he cared about were safe for the moment. Sheriff Jericho Silver had ridden from ranch to ranch along the polluted stream, warning everyone of the danger. Another thirty-six hours and they'd have the outbreak under control.

"Don't go out, Winifred. Even down to the hotel restaurant. Don't drink any water that Sam hasn't boiled first. Even Rosemarie's bathwater should be boiled."

"Strawberries for dessert," Sam announced from the doorway.

Zane laid his fork aside and pushed back his dining chair. "Save mine, Sam. I have to go down to the hospital after supper."

"Will put in cooler with roast chicken chests."

Winifred stifled a burst of laughter.

"Good man," Zane said under his breath. He stood and moved to the front hall. Winifred met him at the door and handed over his leather medical bag. Then she touched his arm.

"I know it's not necessary to warn a physician to be careful, but you will be, won't you?"

He smoothed his free hand over her cheek. "I will be. There are things I want to do before I die."

She shivered. "Don't say that. It's bad luck."

"Ah. How about this, then. There's something I want to do before another day goes by."

"Intriguing," she allowed.

He gave her a long look. "It will be."

She closed the door after him, then carefully opened it again and stood watching his tall, well-knit form stride down the hill to the hospital. *Oh, dear Lord, please keep this man safe.*

"Missy?"

"Yes, Sam, what is it?"

"Yan Li put baby Rose in crib. Which bedroom?"

Winifred shut the door a second time. "Put her in my room, please. When the doctor comes home, he will be very tired and won't want to be disturbed."

\* \* \*

At half past two in the morning, Zane stumbled into the house, dropped his bag in the hallway and washed his hands at the kitchen sink. Then he dragged his aching body up the stairs. A lamp stood on the hall table, turned down low. With a tired sigh, he blew it out and headed into his bedroom. He felt so heartsick he wanted to grind his teeth and weep.

The moon had risen and pale silvery light flooded the room. He kicked off his shoes, but just as he was about to shed the rest of his clothes, a glint of something caught his eye. A china bowl heaped with strawberries sat on his pillow.

Winifred. He'd never been able to resist strawberries. He knew she had brought them up and left them for him. Oh, God. Suddenly he wasn't hungry for strawberries; he was hungry for her.

He padded down to her room, tapped softly on the door and walked in. "Winifred?"

"I am awake, Zane. I couldn't sleep."

He tiptoed past the baby's crib to her bed and bent to touch her cheek.

"Something has happened," he said.

She sat upright, peering into his face. "Your voice sounds so odd. What is it?"

"I lost a patient tonight," he said as evenly as

he could manage. "The Madsen boy. He was only three years old."

"Oh, Zane. I am so very sorry."

"There's more," he said. "I—I need to be with you."

She made no answer, just looked up at him. Then she spoke a single word. "Yes."

He drew back the sheet covering her and bent to slip one hand around her shoulders and the other under her knees, then lifted her into his arms. He stepped quietly around the crib where Rosemarie slept, propping the door ajar so he could hear her if she cried, and made his way down the hall to his own room. He moved to the bed and gently lowered Winifred on top of the quilt.

She wore some kind of soft, almost sheer gown. His fingers hesitated at the top button, then moved instead to his own garments, shucking off everything, his shirt, trousers, drawers. When he was naked, he moved to his bedroom door, cracked it slightly, then lay full length beside her and gathered her close.

"I'm too tired tonight to do what I've been thinking about for months, but I want you to know it's still on my mind." He leaned away from her, retrieved the bowl of strawberries from the floor beside the bed and poked one into his mouth. The sweetness brought tears to his eyes.

"Thank you for these." He offered her a berry. "This means a great deal to me. More than you know. And I'm not talking about these strawberries."

They ate them all, without talking, and when the bowl was empty Zane once more set it on the floor and without a word unbuttoned her nightgown, drew it over her head and tossed it away. Then he pulled her into his arms and tangled his fingers in her hair.

Winifred listened to the night sounds around her, the crickets in the garden below, a frog croaking somewhere, Zane's slow breathing. Her heart swelled into rhythm with his.

His hand on her back fell away and when his breathing slowed, then deepened, she realized he had fallen into an exhausted sleep. It didn't matter. She would still be here when he woke up.

She opened her eyes when the sky was just turning pink. Zane was already awake, propped up on one elbow, looking down at her.

"I regret that I was too worn out to do last night justice," he said, his voice quiet.

"I was relieved, to be honest. I—"

He stopped her words with his mouth. "Don't talk, Winifred." He pushed the sheet covering her down to her waist.

"My God, you are beautiful."

"R-really? I always felt plain next to Cissy."

"You are anything but plain. Winifred, I—"

"Don't you talk, either," she said quickly. "Don't say anything except that you are pleased."

"Pleased! 'Pleased' is eating strawberries in bed. What I am at this moment is overwhelmed."

"Good." She sighed the word. "I want you to be overwhelmed."

"Not yet. There is something I want you to know." He tipped her chin up so their eyes met. "Winifred, I am in love with you. Surely you have guessed this?"

"No. And yes. I did not guess until two days ago when we went swimming. And then what I guessed was that…" She blushed and bit her lower lip. "…that I wanted you to touch me, to kiss me all over. And I could not but think it was because I have come to…" Her voice trailed away.

"To?" he prompted.

"To love you. Oh, Zane, that day I felt something I'd never felt before. It was heavenly."

"Good. I want to be the first. You will never know how much I want it."

He drew her close and began to circle his hand on her bare back.

"Where did you get this scar?"

"Cissy," she whispered. "She hit me with an ice skate."

"Why?" He continued to move his fingers on her skin.

"She wanted to go skating. I wanted to practice the piano. She was impulsive that way."

His hand stopped. "I always suspected in some way that Celeste ran away with me as an act of rebellion."

"Oh, no, Zane. She was wildly in love with you."

He resumed making lazy circles on her skin. "She thought she was in love with me. Later, I realized I'd simply turned her head."

"But you loved her."

"I did. Very much. She gave me the greatest gift a woman can give a man."

"I would never have come to Smoke River if it had not been for Cissy's child," Winifred said quietly. "We would never have met."

"Are you glad we did?"

"Yes."

"When a Klamath or Nez Perce Indian loses a wife, he takes the sister. Did you know that?"

"No, I did not know."

"That, however, is not why you are here with me now." He bent to kiss her and she turned into his embrace.

"I want to be with you," she murmured.

"Are you sure?"

"I am sure."

He propped himself on one elbow and smoothed his hand over her breasts, her soft nipples, then moved to her belly. When he reached the dark hair between her thighs, she sucked in a breath.

"Are you frightened?"

"Not of you, no."

"Of what, then?"

"I do not want to conceive."

His fingers stilled. "Ah. When was your last monthly course?"

"It ended two days ago."

"Then do not be concerned. It is extremely unlikely that you will conceive."

He moved his hand again, lower, touching her with his fingers to ease his entry. Her mouth opened in a moan soft as a breath and she moved convulsively under his touch. He couldn't help smiling. She was responsive beyond his imagining. He wanted her first time to be wondrous for her.

She moved again, stretching toward him, opening her thighs. He put his mouth there and heard her breath catch. He stroked her soft folds with his tongue until she cried out. God, she was wonderful. *Wonderful.*

She grew wet under his mouth, wet and hot and…female. It was the only word that seemed right, and at this moment it seemed very, very right.

He brought his lips to her temple. "Winifred," he whispered. "I want you very much. And I want you now."

He rose over her and caught his breath when she reached her arms around his body and pulled him down to her. He placed her legs farther apart and positioned himself at her entrance.

"Keep your eyes open," he breathed. "Keep looking into mine."

He pressed into her. She was moist and tight and he could tell by her breathing that she was waiting for more. He took it slow, moving deeper a scant inch at a time, feeling her flesh stretch to take him.

Her eyes held his. "Do it now," she murmured. "All of it."

He drew a breath without moving, blew it out and drew another. Then he thrust hard. She caught her breath on a cry and then she was smiling up into his eyes and arching toward him.

He withdrew partway and thrust again, slowly, heard her whispered "yes," and lost himself. Her sheath closed around him in spasms and with surprise he realized that she was climaxing. He moved inside her until he stopped thinking and let himself tumble over the edge into the sweetest oblivion he had ever known.

When he came to himself he could not speak. God, he prayed it had been half as good for her.

He rolled away from her, then pulled her into his arms.

"Winifred, what is between us is serious. You know that, don't you?"

"Yes, I know," she said. Her voice was soft and sleepy and he wanted her all over again.

She ran her fingers down his cheek to his chin. "I think loving someone is beautiful," she murmured.

He caught her hand and pressed his mouth into her palm, then kissed her lips. "I want you to marry me."

Her face changed. "I can't, Zane. I have a career. My teaching. Concerts. Obligations. I've worked hard to establish myself. I can't give that up."

"Why not? Celeste did. She gave it all up when she married me."

Tears filled her eyes. "I am not Cissy. She was my piano duet partner. She did not teach at the conservatory."

He swiped the moisture off her cheeks. "I thought it was different for a woman."

"Perhaps it is for some women," she said. "But…" Her voice hitched. "But not for me. Could you simply move your medical practice to some other town?"

He blinked at the suggestion. "No, of course I could not. I have a partner, Samuel Graham. He and I built the hospital together. And Smoke River is my home."

"But it is not my home. My home is in St. Louis. I am a professor of music at the conservatory there, and I cannot just leave that behind. It matters to me."

"How much does it matter?"

"It matters a lot."

"Winifred, I'm offering you everything I have, everything I am."

"I know, Zane. And it still matters."

## Chapter Sixteen

Winifred heard the crash of the front door and a thump as Zane dropped his medical bag in the hallway. He strode through the dining room and into the kitchen, and the splash of water told her he was scrubbing his hands. When he reappeared, he sank into his place at the dining table with a ragged sigh and dropped his head in his hands.

She stared at him as if he'd dropped from the moon. "Zane? Are you all right?"

"I know I must look awful," he grated. "Haven't slept, haven't shaved in twenty-four hours and my sanity is hanging by a thread."

His face looked gray with fatigue. "Whatever is wrong?"

He groaned. "Two new cases of cholera and an accident at the sawmill. Man lost the fingers of one hand. Damned dangerous blades on those belt saws."

Sam set a large bowl of hearty stew in front of him and a smaller bowl for Winifred. The warm bread that accompanied it she had made herself that morning. She opened her mouth to mention it, then changed her mind. A man this tired hardly cared who baked the bread, or who made the stew or the apple pie they would have for dessert.

He polished off his bowl of stew and Sam instantly refilled it. Zane smiled wearily. "Where is Rosemarie?"

"She's asleep upstairs in my room," Winifred said. "She's fine, Zane. We are all fine. You need not worry about us."

"I worry anyway." His eyes were red-rimmed but his gaze was steady. "Dr. Graham thinks we've got the cholera outbreak under control. We'll know for sure in the next twelve hours if no new cases come in."

"Can you rest before you go back tonight?"

"No. Samuel's there alone and it's too much for one doctor."

To take his mind off the hospital and the grim battle against the cholera epidemic, she told him about Rosemarie's day, how she had gobbled down some cooked carrots and smeared bread dough in her hair—little things that might distract him. He ate while she talked, smiling every now and then.

"Good stew," he said when he finished his second bowl. He looked up at her. "Good bread, too. You make it?"

Winifred nodded. "Sam says my baking is almost as good as Uncle Charlie's."

"I don't suppose there's much you can't do, if you put your mind to it."

"We'll see. I'm in charge of the conservatory's summer concerts in the park this August. I've only performed in them, but I've never been in charge before."

His face changed subtly, the warm light fading from his gray eyes. "August," he repeated. "That's in two weeks."

"One week. I must return early to chair the planning meetings."

He said nothing else, but she knew he was disappointed, that he wanted her to stay until…well, for Zane there was no "until."

He ate four bites of her apple pie and left for the hospital again.

At three in the morning, Zane dragged himself up the stairs and stumbled into his bedroom. Without lighting the lamp he shed his clothes down to his drawers, but when he turned toward the bed he realized he wasn't alone.

"Winifred! What on earth? I didn't expect—"

"I know you didn't. But you looked so tired at supper it decimated my resolve to stay away."

He sank down on the bed beside her. She had on that soft silky gown again, the one with seventeen buttons up the front, and he had to smile. "Oh, my dearest girl," he breathed. He was so exhausted he doubted he could undo a single one.

She pressed her fingers against his lips. "Don't talk, Zane. You need to sleep."

With a groan he shucked his drawers and crawled in beside her. She smelled so good, like violets or roses, or both. He didn't care, as long as it wasn't hospital soap and carbolic.

She reached for him, pulled his head down onto her breast and stroked her fingers through his hair. He hadn't had a chance to shave; maybe it didn't matter.

"Winifred." He murmured her name again and again until he let sleep take him.

Lying close beside him, Winifred felt tears sting behind her eyelids. She loved him. And she couldn't stay in Smoke River.

But she could give him this.

The train back to St. Louis left at four the next afternoon. Winifred laid the last item in her valise and resolutely snapped the lock closed, but she couldn't bring herself to move any faster. She felt as if both legs were weighted down with lead-soled boots.

Slowly she made her way down the staircase to the front hallway to wait for Zane to bring the buggy around.

Sam went up after her luggage and when he returned Yan Li appeared with Rosemarie toddling right behind her. The Chinese girl threw her arms around Winifred.

"You come back, missy. You promise?"

"I promise." She hugged the young woman and turned away as Sam thrust a small wicker hamper into her hands.

"Supper," he announced.

But by far the worst part about leaving was saying goodbye to Rosemarie. Winifred swung her up into her arms and held her tight, burying her nose against the baby's sweet-smelling neck.

"Oh, my darling child, how I will miss you."

Rosemarie clung to her. "'Infred." Winifred pried her tiny hands from around her neck and the baby began to cry. Winifred handed her to Yan Li and the wailing swelled. "'Infred. 'Infred."

Her own tears clogged her throat.

Sam marched through the front door with her valise, set it in the buggy at Zane's feet and then turned, as Winifred came down the porch steps clutching the wicker hamper and her reticule.

"Goodbye, Sam."

"I take good care of Boss. You take good care of you, missy. Come back soon."

Unable to speak over the tightness in her throat, Winifred could only nod. She patted the house-boy's arm, then climbed up beside a somber-faced Zane.

"I hate this," he muttered.

She nodded again and swallowed hard against the sob that rose.

The station platform looked deserted and for one dizzying moment Winifred thought perhaps she had missed the eastbound train. But no, people were crowded into the station house to escape the blazing afternoon sun.

Zane handed her down and motioned to the shaded bench next to the building. They sat side by side without talking while Winifred steeled herself to leave Smoke River.

When the locomotive steamed in, neither of them moved.

Finally Zane stood, picked up her valise and offered his other hand to her. He shoved the leather portmanteau onto the boarding step and only then did he release her fingers.

Her vision blurred with tears. She hesitated,

then pivoted back to him. He caught both her hands to his chest and held them tight.

She longed to twine her arms around his neck but people were beginning to spill out of the station house. Even though he'd kissed her right on the platform when she'd left before, she didn't want to cause too much talk.

Zane stood without moving. She couldn't look at him yet. In a moment she would feel stronger and then— The train whistle split the air. She did look up then, saw his mouth twist, his gray eyes fill with pain.

"Oh, Zane, it is so hard to leave you." Her voice choked off. He dropped her hands and caught her close.

"Don't cry, dammit. I can't stand it."

She did anyway. Tears spilled down her cheeks, wetting his face and the collar of his shirt. The train screeched again.

He pressed his mouth close to her ear. "I love you," he whispered. "And you love me."

Then he turned her toward the passenger car and gave her a gentle push. Clutching the picnic hamper, she walked forward three steps and climbed aboard.

The instant she took a seat in the passenger car she leaned out the open window and the train began to slide on down the track.

Zane stood motionless, watching her glide away from him, until she could no longer see him.

She wept all the way to Idaho.

## *Chapter Seventeen*

August 5th
Dear Zane,
I arrived last night, travel-weary and sad. I miss Rosemarie already, and I began missing you the minute the train pulled out.

I had scarcely unpacked my valise when I was called upon to chair the meeting of the Summer Concert Committee. And, oh, the squabbling! Should we start off with a string quartet or a piano student recital? What will we do if it rains? Which wind quintet first? Flutes and oboes or trumpets with bassoon?

My, how petty musicians can be. Perhaps a conclave of physicians would be equally contentious, though neither you nor your partner Dr. Graham seem anything but co-operative and unflappable.

I dislike being in charge of such quarrelsome factions. In fact I am beginning to dislike the quarrelsome factions!

The weather is perfect for outdoor concerts in the evening, just a touch of breeze to cool the air. August always brings such gorgeous night skies, with stars like silver jewels on dark blue velvet. The usual staff picnics are out of the question because of the humidity, but I plan to go for long walks every evening.

I miss you. I wonder sometimes if we were fated to meet as we did, and to like each other so much. At other times I think God is surely playing a cruel joke. I am bereft, thinking of all that Cissy is missing—Rosemarie's mania for chocolate cookies and bread dough and her dear little sleepy face when she first wakes up in the morning.

I understand more clearly what my sister must have felt when she ran away with you to Smoke River. Practicing Mozart and Brahms must not have seemed important when weighed against not seeing you again.

Tomorrow I must begin to work on the Schubert piano quintet for the second park concert; it has a beastly final movement, full of racing arpeggios and spread-out chords.

Professor Beher, the bassoon player, is stopping in for tea tomorrow afternoon; I will bake chocolate cookies and think of Rosemarie.

And you.

Winifred

August 12th

Dear Winifred,

Your letter reached me at the end of a long afternoon of hospital rounds, during which I thanked whatever God there is that we have no new cholera patients. The last one, Mrs. Madsen, was released this morning.

But about your letter. I read it avidly while Samuel tried to gain my attention; finally he snatched it away and complained, "Well, for heaven's sake, man, if you'd just marry the girl you wouldn't have to write letters!"

Those are his exact words.

I wanted to punch him.

Yan Li and Rosemarie went for a "walk" this morning, mostly to gain some relief for that poor beleaguered cat of Sam's. "Kitty" is now Rose's favorite word. That and "'infred." By the time you return at Christmas she will be able to pronounce your name properly; then she can start on "Nathaniel."

"Daddy" is too easy for a child as intrigued with words as she is. My middle name is Austen; perhaps she might prefer only two syllables.

I admit to being jealous of Professor Bassoon's having tea with you. More than a little jealous, to be honest. I want no other man to share even a teapot with you, or win your admiration, or touch you. Forgive me for this, but I think it characteristic of the male of our species to be possessive.

Of late I find I cannot read poems by Milton, or Tennyson, or Wordsworth, or even the awful doggerel that appears in the *Smoke River Sentinel* every Saturday, written by women who have never been in love.

There is no point in denying how much I miss you. You know I want you in my life, and in my bed. And I know as surely as the sun rises each morning that I will never want anyone else but you.

Rosemarie now sits on my lap as I write this; those sticky chocolate fingerprints on the paper are hers. Well, maybe one very little one is mine.

Come back to us, my darling.

Zane

August 17th

Dear Zane,

Our second concert in the park was a huge
success. The string quartet played brilliantly,
the audience shouted bravos and applauded
until their hands must have ached and afterward the president of the conservatory per-
sonally congratulated me on a "very fine
example of musicianship."

All I wanted to do was return home, take
a cool bath and forget about next Sunday's
concert. It isn't the weather that is oppressive;
it is the strain of getting the violinist and the
cellist to sit down together on the bandstand
without hissing obscenities at each other! I
pray that the trumpet and oboe players will
be better mannered.

What is it that makes people go mad in
the summertime?

I am starting to teach a few new piano
students, but my heart is not in it. These are
youngsters, girls mostly, who failed the entrance exam for conservatory admission
and are attempting to challenge the ruling
against them. I feel sorry for them, really.
But had they worked harder, they would not
be scrambling now.

Cissy would say—well, she did say, and

quite often—that there was more to life than practicing the piano. In some ways I feel I am looking back at myself when I was that age, wondering about the choices I have made in my life.

I am not weary of music, or of playing the piano, or teaching, or of performing on the concert stage. But I am dreadfully tired of the politics of my conservatory and the petty concerns of some prima donnas on the staff.

My friend Millicent is not one of them. I pray that I myself will not turn into one of these.

My spirits are low tonight, as you can no doubt tell. The end of summer is drawing near and with it comes the ennui I always experience before the new term starts. This year there is a great restlessness in me as well. Perhaps I am just growing older. Or perhaps something is shifting within me.

Or perhaps I am simply missing you so profoundly I cannot think clearly.

Winifred

August 30th

Dearest Winifred,

I have surprising and wonderful news. Yan Li is expecting a baby! Yesterday afternoon she fainted in the kitchen as she was washing dishes, and when I examined her—Sam ran all the way to the hospital to get me—there it was: a tiny, very rapid little heartbeat. Sam is so stunned he cannot remember how to scramble eggs, but Yan Li is as unruffled as one of those chickens she has tamed. She should deliver next May.

She wants you to be here for the baby.

I want you to be here for any reason at all.

Winifred, when you left in July I swore to myself I would not beg you to return. I cannot in good conscience ask that you give up the professional career you have established, but, my darling, I cannot lie. I want you here with me. With Rosemarie.

I wish there were some way I could provide what you need for real happiness and fulfillment in your life, but in truth all I, or any man who loves a woman, can offer is himself, his love and his support.

You hold my heart now and forever. I have never loved to the depth and strength of what I feel for you now, not even with Celeste. God forgive me, but it is true.

At night I lie awake and write letters to you in my mind. And during the daylight hours you move always on the edge of my thoughts.

You are always with me. Always.

Zane

## Chapter Eighteen

Winifred surreptitiously ran her thumb along the edge of the large square polished walnut table about which seventeen of her fellow conservatory faculty members gathered. The new term would start next week and during the next three hours the perennial matters of classes and practice rooms and who would first use ensemble rehearsal space would be hashed out.

The conservatory director, Professor Rolf Adamson, lightly tapped his wooden gavel, and conversation dwindled into silence. He began to outline the meeting agenda but Winifred found herself gazing out the tall windows, admiring the bright crimson and gold maple trees along the faculty house walkway. She loved the brilliant colors of fall, and when the leaves withered and left the bare branches shuddering in the winter winds, an inexplicable sadness fell over her spirits.

It was like life, she supposed. Eventually spring would come, bringing new green buds and bright golden jonquils poking up from the earth, but it always saddened her to see a lovely thing pass, even a show of scarlet leaves in the fall, which would soon blow away.

Today it seemed especially difficult to keep her mind on the perennial meeting controversies: Should the string department be awarded an extra rehearsal hall time or should the woodwinds have it? Could the piano teachers take on three advanced pipe organ students or could they wait until next term? And who would manage the recital schedule this year and iron out the continuing squabbles and professional rivalries?

Winifred caught her friend Millicent's keen brown eyes and shared a look of exasperation. Streaks of gray peppered the neat bun at the older woman's nape and the severe navy dress revealed an expanding girth. Millicent was aging, she realized suddenly. Her friend had taught piano at the conservatory for fourteen years.

Winifred caught herself in a sigh. Would she look like Millicent in another seven years? Even three years?

She pressed her lips closed. Did she care whether the oboe professor was now maneuvering the string players out of rehearsal space? Or whether two viola teachers complained about their teaching load?

No, she did not. Again she gazed at the shimmering maple trees outside the window; now back-lit by the afternoon sun, they seemed to glow.

But she did care deeply about her piano students, their recitals, their progress toward proficiency. And she cared passionately about her own performances this season, with Pierre du Fulet conducting her two favorite Beethoven piano concertos; following that, Boston again wanted her for more Mozart recitals and a new Fauré work.

She watched a small brown sparrow hop onto the tree branch closest to the window and cock its head at her as if to say, *Why do you watch me and dream of spring? Are you not content?*

Of course she was content. She was fulfilling the acknowledged purpose of her entire life, what she had worked toward for ten long years.

The oboe professor made a rude remark and everyone laughed, even Rolf Adamson. Everyone except Winifred, who hadn't been listening. A general stirring among those seated around the table alerted her to another simmering controversy, but she found she didn't care until Millicent again caught her eye and raised her eyebrows.

In the next moment Professor Adamson called

for a show of hands: all those in favor of an extra vacation day at Christmas?

Just as Winifred thrust her arm in the air, the door burst open and a young messenger boy entered, waving a telegram. Rolf Adamson snagged it, tipped the lad, then glanced down at the address.

"Miss Von Dannen, this is for you." It was passed down to her, and then everyone resumed the conversation about Christmas vacation.

Winifred ripped open the telegram.

ZANE SERIOUSLY INJURED STOP
COME AT ONCE STOP
DR. SAMUEL GRAHAM

With a cry she started up from her chair. She felt numb, her mind suddenly a dark fog. In an instant Millicent was beside her.

"I must go to Oregon. To Smoke River." She stumbled over the words.

"Now?" Millicent whispered.

With an answering nod, Winifred crumpled the telegram in her hand and moved toward the door.

Millicent followed. "Professor Beher, could you drive Winifred to the train station once she's ready to leave? It's an emergency."

Winifred didn't wait to hear his response but

fled down the hallway, out the conservatory entrance and down the street toward her home. *Oh, dear God, let him be all right. Please, Lord. Please.*

She stepped off the train into a face-nipping wind. She gripped her hat and closed her eyes, her entire body shaking with exhaustion.

"Miss Winifred," a voice shouted. She opened her eyes to see a slim young man striding toward her.

"Sandy Boggs, the sheriff's deputy, remember? Doc Graham sent me to meet your train."

"Oh, Sandy, thank you."

He grabbed up her valise and took her elbow. "Buggy's right here. You wanna go straight to the hospital?"

Winifred nodded.

"Thought you might. I'll drop you there and take your luggage on up to the doc's house. Wing Sam's expecting you."

"How is—?" She couldn't finish the question.

Sandy pursed his lips. "He's still unconscious, ma'am." He loaded her valise and handed her into the buggy, climbed aboard and whipped the horse into a trot. "Been four days now and he hasn't woke up. Doc Graham's waiting for you at the hospital."

Four days! Her heart dropped into her belly.

It all felt unreal. The street, the people, even the white-painted hospital looked just as it always had, but everything was different. Inside that building Zane lay fighting for his life.

She struggled to wrap her mind around what had happened, to stay calm, to be strong. She would not cry. She bit down on her lower lip so hard she tasted blood.

At the hospital, Dr. Graham grasped her elbow. "Thank God you're here, Winifred." He ushered her into a small reception room adjoining the wide entrance hall.

"Before you go in to see him, let me prepare you."

Her stomach clenched. The doctor sat her down in a straight-backed chair and reached for her hand. "It's a head injury. There was an accident at the sawmill. Zane was pulling the man out from under a belt when the log slipped. It caught him across the back of his head."

Winifred sucked in a breath. "Will he live?"

The gray-haired physician hesitated. "Can't say, to be honest. I won't lie to you, Winifred. He hasn't regained consciousness since they brought him in, and the longer he stays that way, the slimmer his chances are."

She pressed her fist against her mouth and bent her head. "May I see him?" she whispered.

Dr. Graham rose and helped her to her feet. "You look done in, my dear. Maybe you should go on up to the house and rest first."

"No. I want to see him."

He nodded, then walked her down the hall to a room with a No Admittance sign on the door, pushed it open and slipped his arm around her shoulders.

She stepped to the single bed and a stifled sob escaped. Zane lay half-covered by a sheet, his chest bare, arms at his sides. But his face— Oh, God. His skin was paste-colored and white gauze bandages swathed his head. His closed eyelids looked bluish and his breathing was very rapid and shallow.

"You can talk to him if you want, Winifred. The last sense to go is hearing, so it's possible he might be able to hear you."

She lifted one of his limp hands. "Zane." Her throat closed. "Zane, it's Winifred. I came as soon as I could."

After a few moments, Dr. Graham gently disengaged Zane's hand from hers and turned her away from the bed. "That's probably enough for right now."

"Isn't there anything else I can do?"

The physician sighed. "Possibly. Just keep talking to him, but first…"

He led her out into the hallway and nodded at a tall older woman in a crisp white smock. The woman sent Winifred an encouraging smile and disappeared into Zane's room.

"First," the physician continued, "you need to rest. Elvira will watch over him."

Numb, Winifred laid her trembling hand on the physician's sleeve. "You will send someone for me if—?"

"I will. You have my word. Now, Sandy's waiting outside with the buggy to drive you home."

How she got through the next hour she didn't know. Sam greeted her at the door with a somber bow and Yan Li tried to smile but kept wiping tears off her cheeks.

But what broke Winifred's heart were Rosemarie's forlorn cries for her papa. She gathered the girl into her arms, then let Sam carry her luggage upstairs. She settled Rosemarie on the bed beside her and tried to sleep.

Hours later she awoke to find Rosemarie gone and a tray of tea and sandwiches on her bedside table. At first she couldn't eat a single mouthful, but then she gave herself a stiff talking to. *You must eat. You must keep up your strength. Do it for Zane and for Rosemarie.*

Later that night she walked down the hill to the hospital and sat by Zane's bed. She tried to do what Dr. Graham had advised, but it was hard to talk over her tears.

"I came on the train from St. Louis, Zane. It took the same three days but this time it seemed much, much longer because—" She broke off and smoothed her fingers over his limp hand.

"Rosemarie is fine. She's getting so big now, isn't she?

"Growing up just like a weed, my father would say. She is a beautiful child, Zane. She asks for you over and over, but I do not think she should see you like this. Later, perhaps, when you can open your eyes and can talk to her. Otherwise it might frighten her."

She paused to steady her voice. It would not help him to hear her cry.

"Dr. Graham says you may be able to hear me, so I'm going to keep on talking." She paused and drew in a shaky breath. "Well, let's see. The conservatory faculty is in its usual uproar over who gets which rooms and what students and the first recital dates. It all seems silly and unimportant to me now that I am here, but I will tell you about it anyway since…since Dr. Graham thinks it may help you."

She stroked his hand, then lifted it to her cheek. "My friend Millicent—I've told you about her, haven't I? She also teaches piano. She helped me pack my valise. I was in such a dither I couldn't think, so it is possible I have brought too many pairs of gloves but no undergarments."

She watched his face for a flicker of life. Nothing. And his breathing remained unchanged.

"Sam is treating Yan Li as if she is made of spun sugar. He won't even let her lift an iron skillet to scramble eggs!"

The nurse, Elvira Sorensen, now fully recovered from her gunshot wound, brought a glass of water for her and Winifred gulped down the contents. Her throat felt dry and scratchy from talking.

She talked until she couldn't keep her eyes open any longer, and then Dr. Graham stepped in and gently guided her out and down the hall. Sandy was waiting to walk her home. Her heart swelled at the kindness of the young deputy, but she couldn't articulate one single word of thanks. He seemed to understand. On the front porch he tipped his Stetson and gave her a thumbs-up sign.

Sam and Yan Li fussed over her and coddled Rosemarie until bedtime. They had set up an extra crib in their room off the kitchen, and Yan Li assured her that Rosemarie was used to sleeping downstairs.

"Baby sleep, no matter what," Sam confided. "Same for you, missy. Must sleep."

The following morning Yan Li made the little pancakes Zane liked so much. Rosemarie had developed a taste for them as well, though more ended up on her face than in her mouth. Winifred picked at her breakfast until Sam stood frowning beside her. "You eat," he ordered. "Yan Li make special."

An hour later Winifred tiptoed into Zane's hospital room to find Dr. Graham bent over him, stethoscope in hand.

At her questioning look he shook his head.

"There's been no change, my dear."

She resumed her place at Zane's bedside and again began to talk. She told him every inconsequential thing she could think of, about Yan Li's pancakes and Rosemarie's ability to smash them back into dough and smear them in her hair; the crisp sunshine outside; the lettuce in Yan Li's garden that was going to seed in the fall heat; even Sam's frowning presence beside her at her breakfast table.

Elvira brought a fresh glass of water and Winifred sipped it and went on talking. Hours later, she stopped to draw a breath and heard a strident voice in the hallway outside.

"I must see Zane! Where is he?"

Winifred's heart stuttered. Darla Bledsoe. What

was she doing here? Zane's hold on life was tenuous at best; Darla would only disturb him.

She rose quickly, walked through the door of the hospital room and stepped into Darla's path.

"Stand aside," the young woman snapped. "I know he's in there."

"I will not stand aside," Winifred replied calmly. "Zane is unconscious. Dr. Graham says he needs complete quiet, and no visitors."

"But you're here! I want to see him."

"No." Winifred put as much steel in her voice as she could muster. "You may not see him."

Darla's face grew mottled. "Why not? I'm closer to him than you are!"

Winifred ignored the comment. "Go home, Darla. If you want to help Zane, then pray for him."

The widow made to push her way past, but Winifred stepped in front of her. "Zane does not want to see you."

"You don't know that," Darla shouted.

Winifred took a deep breath. "I do know that. I am not letting you past this door. You will leave him in peace."

Dr. Graham arrived, took hold of Darla's arm and brusquely ushered her away. Shaking, Winifred returned to Zane's bedside and again took his hand in hers.

Suddenly she felt a gentle but definite pressure against her palm.

"Elvira! Elvira, come quick!"

The nurse barreled into the room, her angular face white. "What's wrong?"

"Zane squeezed my hand! I'm sure of it, he pressed my hand." She began to cry. "D-does that mean he's better?"

"Maybe. Let me get Doc Graham."

Less than a minute later, Zane's partner stepped into the room. He lifted Zane's eyelids and studied his pupils, then slapped his stethoscope onto his bare chest.

"Hmm. You say he squeezed your hand?"

"Y-yes," Winifred sobbed. "I know I didn't imagine it. I stepped outside to speak to Mrs. Bledsoe… I'm afraid our voices were very loud, and when I came back—" She couldn't go on.

"Hmm," Dr. Graham said again. "Glad you got rid of Darla Bledsoe." He bent again over Zane's body.

"Keep talking to him if you can manage it, Winifred. Even if he is very deeply comatose, he can still hear." He shot her a look. "But before you do, I want you to go home and get some rest. You've been here most of the day. Eat something. You're not going to do Zane much good if you collapse."

Winifred nodded. "I will. Just let me stay a few more minutes."

Dr. Graham pulled a gold watch from his pocket. "Five minutes, Winifred. Or I'll come back and carry you up the hill myself." He laid his hand briefly on her shoulder on his way out.

She waited until the door closed behind him. "Zane," she breathed. She lifted his hand again. "I'm going to keep talking to you, and maybe it will drive you crazy, and maybe I will run out of things to say, but I'm going to keep talking until you can answer me." She drew in a shuddery breath.

"Oh, Zane, I refused to let Darla see you. I hope I didn't overstep, but, well, even if I did, I don't care."

She pressed his hand to her forehead and brushed tears off her cheeks with her free hand.

And then he squeezed her fingers again.

Four hours later Winifred returned to the hospital to find Elvira Sorensen waiting for her in the entryway, mopping at her eyes with a sodden handkerchief. Winifred's heart rolled up into her throat.

"He's dead, isn't he?" Oh, God, she couldn't bear it.

Elvira enfolded her into her muscular arms. "Oh, no, dear, he's not dead. An hour ago he opened his eyes. He really did! I think he was disappointed to see my face and not yours, but he looked right at me and tried to smile."

Zane cracked open one eyelid and immediately snapped it shut. Blinding sunlight poured in the window and waves of pain washed over the back of his head. Where the hell was he?

Then he heard Elvira Sorensen's scratchy voice. "Zane? Zane, can you hear me?"

A groan was the only sound he could produce. He hoped she understood.

"Zane, you're in the hospital. There was an accident at the sawmill and Ike Bruhn was pulled into a belt saw. When they stopped it, you pulled him away and the log rolled over onto you. Do you remember any of this?"

He shook his head once and wished he hadn't. His skull felt like the entire sawmill had smashed into it. Elvira was snuffling, and that was odd. All his nurses were trained to hide their emotions; he'd have to speak to her about the lapse.

He'd swear he had heard Winifred's voice, but he must have dreamed it. Did he also dream that he heard an argument between Winifred and Darla Bledsoe? Winifred's words had made him want to cheer, but he found he couldn't utter a sound.

He felt Elvira move away from him. Someone else was in the room, but he couldn't tell who it was. Doc Graham?

No. Whoever this was smelled good.

Then he heard Winifred's voice again. "Zane." That was all she said, but it was enough. With an effort he opened both eyes and squinted against the light.

Her face was blurry, but her touch on his hand was real enough. He tried to say her name.

"Zane, you are going to be all right. I know you are." Her voice sounded so calm, so sure. He prayed to God she was not lying to him. His right temple felt like it was exploding and he couldn't keep his eyelids open.

"Head hurts," he managed to say. "Get Samuel."

He sensed her leave his bedside and heard the door open. "Get Dr. Graham," she said to someone. A moment later someone bent over him and he smelled the antiseptic of Graham's hospital smock. A cold stethoscope settled on his chest.

"Samuel," he murmured. "Bad headache."

"Small wonder," the physician muttered. "I'll get some laudanum."

Winifred settled again by Zane's bedside, listening to his ragged breathing. She knew he was in pain; his almost bloodless lips were pressed into a thin line and one hand opened and closed convulsively. Dr. Graham returned with a half glass of something in his hand and helped Zane to raise his head and swallow it down.

"How's Ike?" Zane murmured.

Dr. Graham straightened. "His arm's broken in two places. But you'll like this, Zane. His wife's expecting. Ike said if it's a boy he's going to name him after you."

A fleeting smile curved Zane's mouth. "Austen," he muttered. "Nathaniel hard to say."

The door closed behind him, and Winifred tried to stop the tears stinging her eyes. Dear God, would he really recover? She watched his bare chest rise and fall as his breathing slowed. His tense mouth began to relax and the frown creasing his forehead smoothed out.

She brushed her lips lightly against the cool skin of his cheek, then let her head droop forward until it rested against his rib cage. His hand settled against her hair.

"You really are here," he said, his words slurring. "Thought I was dreaming."

She couldn't answer. Behind her the door opened and Elvira tiptoed in and touched her shoulder. "Come and rest, Miss Von Dannen. I'll make some tea."

Winifred nodded, swiped at the tears coursing

down her cheeks and followed the nurse into the hallway.

"Doc Graham thinks the worst is over."

The nurse's words brought a fresh onslaught of weeping and while the water heated in the tiny nurse's room, Elvira joined her in a good cleansing cry.

The following morning Winifred stepped into the hospital entryway to find Rooney Cloudman pacing up and down outside the door to Zane's room, a bouquet of yellow roses in his gnarled hand. He thrust them at her.

"These are for you, Miss Winifred."

She buried her nose in the blooms. "Oh, Rooney, they are beautiful."

"I heard about what you said to Darla Bledsoe t'other day. Just wanted you to know you done right."

Winifred gulped. "Perhaps I shouldn't have stopped her that way, but I just couldn't... Heavens, it's probably all over town."

"Yep, it's all over town all right. Haven't heard so much cheering since Thad MacAllister brought in his bumper wheat crop last summer."

Winifred's face heated. "I should not have presumed."

"Aw, now, Miss Winifred." He laid his arm

across her shoulders and squeezed. "Me and Sarah, we think you should presume all to hell."

Winifred laughed in spite of herself. When a chuckling Rooney left the hospital, she entered Zane's room and received her second shock of the morning. Zane was propped halfway up in bed, laboriously spooning oatmeal into his mouth.

"Oh, Zane! You're sitting up."

"Damn right. Head still aches, but—" He broke off to drag in a breath and plunged his spoon into the bowl. Winifred noticed his hand was shaking. She reached to take the utensil.

"I can feed you, Zane."

He batted her hand away. "No. It's good practice."

He ate so slowly Winifred gritted her teeth to keep from snatching the bowl away. "Good practice for what?"

"For coming home. Not an invalid."

She noticed his frown deepening and guessed his headache was back. Still he doggedly finished the oatmeal, slid down on the pillows and closed his eyes with a sigh.

"Get Samuel, will you?"

Dr. Graham administered another dose of laudanum, and Zane slept. Winifred read some Wordsworth, paced up and down the hallway outside his room, had tea with Elvira and sat by Zane's bedside and read until her eyes burned.

Late in the afternoon she looked up to find Zane watching her.

"Who brought the roses?" he asked, tipping his chin at the vase on the side table.

"Rooney Cloudman. I was so touched I forgot to ask about their honeymoon trip."

One of Zane's eyebrows rose. "None of our business."

"It seems everything that happens in this town is everybody's business." But she decided not to tell him of the gossip circulating about her encounter with Darla.

"Tell me about Rosemarie. Is she all right?"

"She is just fine. Sam and Yan Li keep her entertained, but she asks and asks where her papa is."

"What do they tell her?"

"They say you are…traveling."

"Good."

"I think it might reassure her to see you."

"No. Don't want her to see me like this. Might frighten her."

"But—"

"Don't." He almost snapped out the word, and Winifred was torn between joy that he had enough energy and breath to do so and annoyance at his order.

She drew in a slow, calming lungful of air and folded her hands in her lap. "I suppose it is a good sign that you are—"

"Bad-tempered?" he inserted.

"Irascible. You are never like this, Zane. Do you want some more laud—?"

"No."

She rolled her eyes. "Goodness, one would never mistake you for a soft-spoken man, now would they?"

Zane just groaned.

"Really, Zane, don't you think—?"

"Dammit, Winifred, I'm not used to being sick."

"You're not 'sick,' Dr. Dougherty. According to Doc Graham, you have had a severe head trauma."

"Hate being down," he grumbled.

Winifred resisted the impulse to laugh. It was the first and only time she'd ever seen a chink in the gentlemanly good humor Zane always exhibited. Maybe it was a good thing for him to realize he was as human as everyone else. That even a physician had vulnerabilities.

But enough was enough.

## Chapter Nineteen

The next afternoon Winifred rebelled. Yan Li dressed Rosemarie in a ruffled pink pinafore, and hand in hand Winifred walked Zane's daughter down to the hospital and into Zane's room. He was sitting in a chair by the window and Rosemarie made straight for him.

"Papa! Papa!"

Winifred lifted her onto his lap. Zane clasped his young daughter in his arms and held her tight. Over her pink pinafore-covered shoulder, he caught Winifred's eye and tried to frown. Then he tried to smile and couldn't do that, either. A fist closed around her heart.

Zane closed his eyes and rocked Rosemarie to and fro, murmuring things Winifred couldn't hear while Rosemarie played with the buttons on his pajama top and chattered on and on in a spate of nonsense syllables. Zane responded as if they made perfect sense.

Finally he set her onto the floor and she toddled over to Winifred and threw her little arms around her knees. "Up," she demanded.

Winifred shot a look at Zane and caught her breath. His gray eyes were wet and shiny. Oh, dear Lord, had she done the right thing in bringing his daughter? Zane had been so…so… Well, lately it was hard to know what was best to do.

Rosemarie sat on her lap, playing with the buttons of the blue dimity shirtwaist she'd donned this morning, until she grew drowsy. She lifted the baby to kiss Zane, took her tiny hand and walked back up the hill to the house for lunch and a nap.

When she returned to the hospital that evening, Zane was wide awake and waiting for her.

"Tell me about you, Winifred," he said with no preamble.

"Me?"

"How is it that you are here?"

"On the train, as usual. That seems an odd question from someone who's met my train on a number of occasions."

"I mean, why did you come?"

She stiffened. "Zane, I cannot believe you are asking this. I came because Samuel wired me had been injured."

"Ah," he said.

"Oh, Zane, I came because I couldn't bear to *not* be here."

"Better," he breathed. "Much better. Kiss me, Winifred. Gently. My head aches if I move it."

She bent and softly pressed her mouth to his and heard him make a small noise deep in his throat.

"Now," he murmured, "keep on talking."


Zane had walked halfway up the hill from the hospital before he realized he'd pushed too far, too fast. He stopped and puffed hard for a few minutes.

*What am I trying to prove?*

That he was still young and strong and could recover from a head trauma. That he didn't give up without a fight. That he'd be damned if he'd be cooped up in a hospital room for one more hour on this glorious fall morning.

He moved slowly forward. The air smelled of burning leaves and fresh bread from Uncle Charlie's bakery. He dragged in a deep breath and sent up a quiet prayer of thanks that he was alive and well. Relatively well, anyway. At least he would be in a day or two.

That thought stopped him cold a scant three yards from his front porch steps. When Doc Gra-

ham assured her Zane was well, Winifred would
return to St. Louis. His chest ached at the knowl-
edge.

It was pure hell saying goodbye to her after
each visit to Smoke River. After she climbed on
that train and rolled away from him he couldn't
sleep for days afterward. Or eat. Or stop thinking about her.

He forced his legs to carry him up the six steps,
and sank his shaking frame onto the porch swing.
His pulse pounded, but at least his head didn't
ache.

Samuel told him he was lucky he hadn't woken
up blind or unable to talk or impaired in some
other way from a brain injury. He wondered if he
could still make love.

Might be too soon to explore that possibility.

He leaned his head back against the cushion and
thought about it. Under the freshly laundered and
ironed shirt he'd borrowed from Samuel he could
feel sweat rolling down his chest. Elvira confessed
she had burned his own shirt after the accident. He
wore his own trousers; at least they hadn't been
blood-soaked. The knee was ripped, though. Wing
Sam could mend it.

The smell of coffee drifted to his nostrils and
suddenly he was hungry for anything as long as
it wasn't hospital oatmeal. Maybe Yan Li would

make those little flavorful pancakes. He'd try standing up in another minute; if he could make it through the front door, he could feed Rosemarie her breakfast.

A smile tugged at his mouth. He slipped inside the house and dropped quietly into his chair at the head of the dining table. From the kitchen came the soft chatter of Sam and Yan Li, punctuated by the clank of pots and the hiss of the teakettle on the woodstove.

*Dear God in heaven, thank You for my life.*

Sam stepped in to lay out plates and napkins and swallowed a cry of surprise. "Boss! What you doing here?"

"Waiting for breakfast," Zane said as calmly as he could.

Yan Li appeared behind Sam and gave a yelp. "Oh! Oh!" she cried. She clapped her small hand over her mouth and tears sparkled in her dark eyes.

"Missy upstairs with daughter," Sam volunteered. "You want coffee?"

"I want coffee all right. Lots of it."

Sam disappeared into the kitchen and after a moment Yan Li stepped forward and set a plate and a cup and saucer before him. "Very glad to see you," she said softly. "I make pancakes?"

Zane could only nod. Damn but it was wonderful to be home, hearing his daughter's prattle from upstairs, and Winifred's quiet responses. One of these days maybe he'd understand more of Rosemarie's rapid-fire sentences. Winifred's were clear enough, but he wondered how on earth she knew what Rose was chattering about.

And then there she was in the doorway, radiant in a yellow shirtwaist and a dark skirt. "Zane!"

He tried to rise to his feet but gave up. His legs were still trembling after the climb up the hill. "I'd get up, Winifred, but I don't think I can."

"Are you crazy? However did you get here?"

"Walked. I've been practicing. Every time Samuel left the hospital I walked up and down the halls."

Rosemarie squealed and wanted to crawl into his lap, so he bent to lift her up. She twined her tiny hands into the overlong hair at his neck and he laughed with pleasure despite his burgeoning headache.

Sam brought coffee, filled their cups and disappeared into the kitchen. They drank in silence, listening to the baby's stream of unintelligible syllables.

"Oh, Zane, it is so good to hear you laugh."

"It's good to be able to laugh without my head feeling like a rocket's gone off inside. I've never been more aware of the blessings in my life."

"It is unfortunate one has to get himself almost

killed to gain such a perspective," she said drily. "Now that you are well, or almost well, I can allow myself to feel all the anger and fear I've stuffed down over the past seven days."

Zane set his coffee cup carefully onto the matching saucer. "Anger about what, Winifred? I am well aware the new term must have started at your conservatory."

"Yes, it has. A week ago."

"And you are missing it." He couldn't look at her, afraid of what he would see in her face.

"I...I sent the director a telegram."

Zane lifted his cup, cradled it in both hands and waited. He didn't think he could stand letting her go back to St. Louis, at least not until he was stronger.

Maybe never. What the hell kind of life was this with Winifred in St. Louis and him here in Smoke River?

No life at all.

"I can't ask you what you said in that telegram. Don't tell me now. Let me have just a bit more time with you without knowing when it has to—"

Winifred sent him an oddly naked look and his breath stopped.

"Rooney Cloudman mentioned the Jensens' harvest dance, this Saturday, Zane. Do you think you will feel up to going?"

"What day is today?"

"Tuesday."

Four days. He'd give anything to dance with Winifred again, hold her close in his arms and feel her warmth against his body. "I'll be there."

A deeper, unspoken question lay between them and Zane knew she wondered about that, too. He wondered about it, as well. But by God if he could dance in four days, he might be able to…

There was no way to practice for what he had in mind, he acknowledged with a wry smile. He'd just have to wait and see.

Winifred watched Zane stagger in with a double load of firewood and dump it in the kitchen wood box with a thump. She tried to tamp down her fury at his pushing himself. At this rate he would be back in the hospital by Saturday, not at the Jensens' barn social.

The man was maddening. He refused to listen when she urged him to rest, avoided any mention of the headaches she knew still plagued him and resolutely shut his ears at her cautionary remarks.

Sam took her aside after breakfast, his face worried.

"Boss do too much, missy."

"I know, Sam. But just try and stop him. Zane is more stubborn than…than…"

"Bull ox," the Chinese man supplied.

"Two bull oxen," she added in exasperation.

Sam lifted his hands in a gesture of resignation and headed back to the kitchen. Winifred stepped into the library, opened the volume of Sir Walter Scott and pretended to read.

Rosemarie was napping. Zane, too, should be resting, but instead he plopped down in his favorite wingback chair opposite her and waited until she glanced up.

"I'm going swimming."

"Whaaat?"

"I said I'm going swimming. Alone."

She stared at him. "Why?"

"Why am I going swimming or why am I going alone?"

She clapped the book closed. "Both," she retorted.

"Because I need to swim laps to build up my strength and because I won't want you nagging at me to stop."

"When have I ever nagged at you?" Her voice, she noted, had gone up an octave.

"It's true you don't nag, Winifred. But you would this time, and I don't have the energy to both swim and argue with you."

Fury swamped her reason. "You are the most unreasonable, difficult, pigheaded—"

He stood up suddenly, seized her by the shoulders and pulled her out of her chair. "Tomorrow's Saturday. I intend to dance with you. All night." He caught her face in his hands and kissed her, hard.

"At least take the buggy, Zane," she said when she could breathe again.

"Nope. I'm taking the horse. Need the exercise." He kissed her again, more slowly. "Go ahead and nag, Winifred. I'm getting to like it."

Out at the swimming hole he swam twenty laps, rested an hour, then swam another twenty. He was dead tired afterward, but he wasn't sorry. If Winifred had come with him he would have spent all his time looking at her and forgotten why he needed to do this.

Tomorrow night at Jensens' dance he would look his fill.

# *Chapter Twenty*

Zane drove the buggy out to the Jensen place on Saturday evening. The balmy evening air smelled of some kind of spicy roses and Winifred looked so enticing in the low-necked pale blue gown it made his heart hurt.

His body was strong enough for anything tonight; the question that nagged him was whether he was strong enough to let her go back to St. Louis afterward.

He'd been careful not to ask about her leaving, not to press her on the matter for fear he would hear something he wasn't ready to hear. But he couldn't stand not knowing much longer. He had to have an answer soon.

Tin can lanterns lit the path to the barn door. Inside it was a jumble of noise and potluck supper aromas and the raucous sound of the musicians—two fiddles, a guitar and a banjo, and the familiar washtub bass plucked by a shiny-faced Whitey Poletti. Children raced around the perimeter of the polished plank floor and young mothers sat on the sidelines nursing babies and gossiping.

A very pregnant Nellie Bruhn, Ike's wife, clung to the plaster cast protecting her husband's broken arm. Zane said a silent prayer that she would not go into labor tonight. He had other things to do besides help a new life into the world.

"Cider, Doc?" Rooney Cloudman stood behind the plank bar.

"Sure."

"Hard or soft?"

Zane glanced across the room where Winifred stood surrounded by Leah MacAllister, Sarah Cloudman and Ellie Johnson. Winifred outshone every woman in the room.

"Hard, Rooney. Make it a double." Suddenly he remembered that first Christmas dance, when he'd first begun to realize he had feelings for Winifred. Feelings, hell. He'd wanted her so much his groin had ached.

As it did now.

Rooney's salt-and-pepper eyebrows rose, but he poured four fingers of dark amber liquor into a glass and handed it over. Zane sipped and circled the room. Sooner or later Winifred would look at him, and then he'd pull her away from her circle of admirers and hold her in his arms.

Sheriff Jericho Silver sat on the sidelines with his wife and their handsome twin boys. Zane saluted her with his glass. Lucky man, Jericho. Or Johnny, as the townspeople called him. Running for judge in next summer's election. Life moved on.

By next summer Sam and Yan Li would have a new baby and…

And what? Where would Winifred be? Here, with him? Or back East at the conservatory with a dozen piano students and a concert series?

He found himself gravitating toward her, and all at once she looked up and saw him. She'd done her hair differently tonight, longer, with more waves at her neck. He wanted to lace his fingers through it.

He cut through the gaggle of people around her and drew her away. "Come with me." Halfway across the room he swung her into his arms.

"Thank you," she breathed. "I was drowning." She reached for the glass of cider he still held in one hand, tipped it up and drained it. Tears came to her eyes.

Zane chuckled.

"I always do that," she gasped. "I forget it isn't lemonade."

"I can get some lemonade for you if you like."

"No. I would rather dance with you."

His breath stopped. "Thank God," he murmured near her ear.

Suddenly the air between them was charged. And just as suddenly Zane found himself terrified that this—tonight—would not go as he hoped.

He lifted the cider glass out of her hand, set it on a bench at the edge of the dance floor and folded Winifred into his arms. Doubtless she could feel his heart thumping under his white linen shirt, but she said nothing, just glanced up at him with a mysterious smile in her eyes.

He wanted to stop right there and kiss her senseless. And then take her straight home to his bed.

She must have heard his groan because she halted abruptly and looked up again. "Zane? What is wrong?"

Everything was wrong. He loved her. Wanted her. And he knew that as soon as he could dance a whole evening of reels and waltzes, as soon as he was strong enough after getting smacked in the head by a log twice the thickness of any man in this room, as soon as he was fully recovered, she would get on the train back to St. Louis. When she thought he didn't need her any longer, she would leave him.

"What is it?" she repeated.

He couldn't answer. "Nothing is wrong," he lied. "Just dance with me."

She lifted her arms. He caught both her hands and pressed them to his chest, curling the fingers of one hand over them to hold them against his thudding heart. He curved his left arm around her back and breathed in the scent of her hair. Lilacs and something sweet, honeysuckle? He moved his hand to press her face into his neck, then slid his fingers up her spine.

"Zane," she whispered. "People are watching us."

"Let them watch."

He didn't speak again until the fiddles struck up a reel and couples lined up opposite each other. He hated to let her go, but he enjoyed watching her from across the expanse of plank floor separating the line of dancers. Her cheeks were flushed and she was smiling across into his eyes. If he lived to be a hundred, he would remember this moment and the look on her face.

The lines advanced toward each other, bowed to their partners and then retreated. He and Winifred were the head couple. They met again in the center of the floor and he grasped her tight and swung her around and around, then released her. It was the last thing he wanted to do.

And when she danced again into the center and

Thad MacAllister swung her, Zane shut his eyes.
He wanted no man to lay his hands on her, not
even his very married friend Thad. Primal male
jealousy, he guessed. He might laugh at himself
if he didn't feel so possessive of the treasure that
Winifred was. If he could be sure she was truly
his and not the coveted darling of some music professor back East.

He wondered why he'd never been like this
about Celeste. He knew he had loved her, but it
had been a young love, one born of enchantment
and losing his head. What he felt for Winifred was
different. More gradual. More real.

And deeper.

That was why it was so important.

He lasted through the reel, four or five two-
steps and another reel before he had to call it quits.
It wasn't his strength that was giving out, it was his
capacity for torturing himself. She was so close,
held in his arms, smiling up at him, her eyes soft,
but still it wasn't close enough.

One more slow waltz, he decided. Just one.

He very nearly didn't make it to the end. His
pulse wouldn't calm down to a manageable rate;
his groin ached so much he fought against dancing her outside and pressing her hard against his
swollen member.

She rested her forehead against his shoulder,

humming along with the fiddles as they sobbed their way through "Red River Valley."

He jerked them to a stop. "Let's go. I'm taking you home."

Without a word, she nodded and went to gather up her lacy blue shawl. She stopped to speak to Sarah Cloudman and Leah MacAllister, then to admire Jericho and Maddie Silver's one-year-old twins. Finally, *finally*, she returned to where Zane waited by the barn entrance. With a final smile and a wave, she took his arm and then they were outside in the soft autumn night.

The moon rose high, washing the road with silvery light and illuminating Winifred's face. After a mile or so she scooted closer and laid her head on his shoulder.

He reined the horse to a halt and pulled her into his arms.

"Kiss me," she whispered. She lifted her face.

They shared two of the most shattering kisses he'd ever experienced. He couldn't tell who was trembling harder, Winifred or himself.

He lowered his mouth to the bare skin above the neckline of her dress and breathed in her scent. She moaned softly and he tore himself away and lifted the reins. It was time for everything he'd planned all these long weeks.

He drove the buggy around to the back of the

house, unhitched the horse and fed it a handful of oats while Winifred lingered on the back stoop. Praying that Rosemarie was asleep in Sam and Yan Li's room, he tiptoed in the back kitchen door, holding Winifred's hand tight in his. He said nothing until they reached the top of the stairs, then he gently turned her to face him.

"I want you to stay with me tonight."

She reached both arms around his neck and kissed his cheek. "Oh, Zane, I thought you would never ask."

She slipped his top shirt button free, and with a stifled sound he scooped her up and kneed open his bedroom door. Setting her on her feet he reached behind her to turn the lock.

"Were we as scandalous at the dance tonight as I felt?" she murmured.

"Probably, yes. Do you care?"

"No. I felt idiotically happy all evening, dancing with you."

He began undoing the buttons of her dress. They ran all down the front to her hemline, but when he reached those below her waist she skimmed the gown over her hips and let it drop to the floor.

"Scandalous," she whispered. "Such a wonderful feeling."

He pressed his lips to her temple, behind her

ear, to the soft, fine skin of her neck, and her breathing stuttered. "Scanda—"

Zane laughed gently and caught Winifred's mouth under his. Oh, mercy, she thought. He had never kissed her like this before. He urged her lips open and she suddenly felt hot all over, as if thousands of stars were dancing on her skin.

He untied the ribbon of her camisole without lifting his head and she heard his murmur of approval that she wore no corset. Surely he'd known that all evening, as close as he had held her.

He shrugged off his shirt, then brought her hands to rest on the belt at his waist. "Scandalous?" he suggested.

She unhooked the metal buckle and tugged down his trousers, waited while he shed shoes and socks and then skimmed his drawers off over his hips. She stepped out of her petticoat and bent to remove her stockings but he stopped her.

He lifted her, set her down on his bed and knelt before her. Slowly he rolled the thin lisle stockings over her knees and down her calves. Her flesh prickled when his fingers grazed her skin. His touch made her feel more than scandalous; it made her dizzy with wanting.

He swung her bare legs onto the quilt and began removing her hairpins, one by one, until her hair fell in waves around her bare shoulders. He wove his fingers into the curly mass, then stretched out full length beside her and began smoothing his hands over every inch of her body—her rib cage, her breasts, her thighs, moving in slow circles and following the path of his fingers with his mouth. He licked a slow path over her throbbing nipples and she sucked in her breath.

"Do you like that?"

"Yes." Her voice was unsteady. On impulse she ran her tongue over his bare chest, across his flat brown nipples.

"Do you?"

"God, yes," he whispered. "Oh, God, yes."

He slid down, rested his palm over her mound and waited. "And this?"

More dancing stars. Millions more. She had never felt anything as glorious as Zane's hands touching her. He slipped one finger inside her and she cried out. She heard his low, satisfied chuckle and that made her bold.

She brushed her fingers over his member and he hissed in a sudden breath and lifted her hand away.

"Do you not like me to touch you?" she asked.

"I do. Right now I like it too much." He bent forward and slid his hot tongue back and forth across her entrance. Again she cried out.

"Winifred," he said, his voice low and rough.

"I want you more than I've ever wanted anything. I'm so in love with you I can't see straight."

He rose over her, positioned himself and filled her with one swift thrust.

"I am yours, Zane. You know that." She sought his mouth and rose to meet his thrusts.

"I don't know how to survive without you," he said against her lips. His movements were slow and deep but she could tell by his breathing he was at the edge of losing control. Instinctively she tightened her muscles around him and suddenly he stopped moving.

He panted for a few seconds and then thrust hard.

She was climbing, reaching for that exquisite pleasure she had felt before with him, and then she was floating, soaring on the crest of something shattering.

Zane caught her cry under his mouth and then he thrust deep and called her name. She clung to him, sobs racking her body. He brushed her hair off her forehead, kissed her eyelids, her face.

"Why are you crying? Did I hurt you?"

"Oh, no. I felt… I don't know, something just welled up inside." She reached up and pulled him down to her. "Don't move," she whispered. "Stay inside me."

"Scandalous," he breathed.

"Yes. It was not like this before, Zane."

He moved to roll off her but she wrapped both arms around him and held on tight. "Don't stop."

"Winifred, I need to rest."

She smiled up at him. "For how long?"

He laughed, and then sobered. "Ten minutes?"

"Too long," she sighed.

He moved off her anyway. "Winifred, there's something I need to say to you."

"Yes?"

"I—I don't think I can stand it when you go back to St. Louis."

"Do you want me to stay?"

His entire body jerked. "Yes, of course I want you to stay. I didn't want to press you, but—"

"Press me," she murmured.

Zane wrapped her in his arms and lay still, trying to digest her words.

"You know that I love you," he said at last.

She nodded.

"And I think…at least I thought, that you loved me."

She nodded again.

"Winifred, look at me. This is serious. You know that, don't you? I'm about to propose marriage to you."

"Yes," she acknowledged.

He stuffed down his frustration. "Shall I proceed?"

Her smile flickered. "Oh, yes, Zane. Please do."

He drew in a deep breath and steeled himself to get his heart broken.

"Winifred, I do know that your music career at the conservatory is important to you. But I can't lose you. Ever. I'm asking you to marry me. To stay here in Smoke River and be my wife."

He held his breath while she smoothed her hand across his cheek. "Yes, my career at the conservatory is important to me. Very important. I have worked for it all my life. But…"

She brushed her thumb over his lower lip. "But it is not as important to me as you are."

"What?" He wasn't sure he'd heard right. "What do you mean?"

"It's simple, Zane. I love you. I want to be here, with you. And Rosemarie. The cost would be too high to miss this during my lifetime."

"Why the hell didn't you tell me?"

"I told you I sent a telegram to the conservatory director."

"Yes, I remember. You didn't tell me what you said in that telegram, however."

"I wired my resignation. I knew the minute I saw you lying in that hospital bed that I'd never be able to leave you again."

"I asked you to marry me the last time you were here," he reminded her.

"I remember. But I wasn't ready then. Then I didn't think I could give up my conservatory career. Now I know it is you I cannot give up."

With a shaky sigh he gathered her close, and after a number of kisses they made love again. And again.

In the morning, a smiling Sam and Yan Li moved quietly about the house, careful not to disturb the couple sleeping behind Zane's bedroom door.

Zane stood quietly at Celeste's grave, Rosemarie's tiny hand clasped in his. Very deliberately he knelt and laid a bouquet of yellow roses on the soft earth.

Someone had planted flowers of some kind, daisies he guessed; they spilled over the site and twined up the gray headstone. Perhaps Winifred had thought to do this.

He plucked a single golden bloom and nestled it behind his daughter's ear. Then he lifted her into his arms and turned toward the small, peaceful town and the road that led home.

# *Epilogue*

❦

*Smoke River Sentinel*
December 24th, 1873

### BELOVED PHYSICIAN MARRIES!
Dr. Nathaniel (Zane) Dougherty was joined in matrimony on Sunday with the former Winifred Von Dannen of St. Louis at a candlelight ceremony at the doctor's Smoke River residence.

The bride wore a simply cut gown of yellow *peau de soie* and carried a bouquet of honeysuckle and yellow damask roses. She was given away by Rooney Cloudman and preceded to the altar by her niece, Rosemarie Winifred Dougherty. Dr. Samuel Graham stood up with the groom, and Reverend Anthony Pollock conducted the service.

Dr. Dougherty is cofounder of the Samuel Graham Hospital and a respected physician and surgeon in private practice, serving both the Smoke River and Gillette Springs communities. The new Mrs. Dougherty was a respected concert pianist and professor of music at the Adamson Conservatory in St. Louis, Missouri.

Following the ceremony, a spectacular seven-layer wedding cake, created by Ming Cha, owner of Uncle Charlie's Bakery, was served along with lemonade and champagne punch.

The couple will reside in Smoke River, where Mrs. Dougherty intends to open a music school.

*Smoke River Sentinel*
January 30th, 1874

NEW MUSIC ACADEMY OPENS!
Winifred (Von Dannen) Dougherty announced the opening of her new music academy at a tea hosted by Sarah Rose Cloudman at Rose Cottage. Private lessons at the school will be offered in piano, violin and voice; in addition, classes will be offered in choral performance and in rhythm band for chil-

dren. Mrs. Dougherty has expressed interest in locating a teacher of both violin and woodwind instruments.

In the fall, Winifred Dougherty will be performing concerts with both the Portland and San Francisco symphony orchestras and she will be presenting recitals with various chamber groups in those cities.

Classes at the new music academy will be held in the upstairs rooms over the new Smoke River Bank & Trust Building.

* * * * *

# REQUEST YOUR FREE BOOKS!

**HARLEQUIN®**

## HISTORICAL

### Where love is timeless

## 2 FREE NOVELS PLUS 2 FREE GIFTS!

**YES!** Please send me 2 FREE Harlequin® Historical novels and my 2 FREE gifts (gifts are worth about $10). After receiving them, if I don't wish to receive any more books, I can return the shipping statement marked "cancel." If I don't cancel, I will receive 6 brand-new novels every month and be billed just $5.69 per book in the U.S. or $5.99 per book in Canada. That's a savings of at least 12% off the cover price! It's quite a bargain! Shipping and handling is just 50¢ per book in the U.S. and 75¢ per book in Canada.* I understand that accepting the 2 free books and gifts places me under no obligation to buy anything. I can always return a shipment and cancel at any time. Even if I never buy another book, the two free books and gifts are mine to keep forever.

246/349 HDN GH2Z

Name _____ (PLEASE PRINT) _____

Address _____ Apt. # _____

City _____ State/Prov. _____ Zip/Postal Code _____

Signature (if under 18, a parent or guardian must sign) _____

### Mail to the **Reader Service:**
**IN U.S.A.:** P.O. Box 1867, Buffalo, NY 14240-1867
**IN CANADA:** P.O. Box 609, Fort Erie, Ontario L2A 5X3

**Want to try two free books from another line?**
**Call 1-800-873-8635 or visit www.ReaderService.com.**

* Terms and prices subject to change without notice. Prices do not include applicable taxes. Sales tax applicable in N.Y. Canadian residents will be charged applicable taxes. Offer not valid in Quebec. This offer is limited to one order per household. Not valid for current subscribers to Harlequin Historical books. All orders subject to credit approval. Credit or debit balances in a customer's account(s) may be offset by any other outstanding balance owed by or to the customer. Please allow 4 to 6 weeks for delivery. Offer available while quantities last.

**Your Privacy**—The Reader Service is committed to protecting your privacy. Our Privacy Policy is available online at www.ReaderService.com or upon request from the Reader Service.

We make a portion of our mailing list available to reputable third parties that offer products we believe may interest you. If you prefer that we not exchange your name with third parties, or if you wish to clarify or modify your communication preferences, please visit us at www.ReaderService.com/consumerchoice or write to us at Reader Service Preference Service, P.O. Box 9062, Buffalo, NY 14240-9062. Include your complete name and address.

HH15

In the darkness, she reached up to Raine's face, touching his cheek. She explored the smooth surface, fascinated by him. He caught her hand and drew her fingers back to her lips in a warning to be still and silent.

The risk of being discovered was far too high. She knew that—and yet, she was tempted to seize a moment to herself. He was only going to push her away as soon as they were out of hiding. She wanted to embrace every last chance to live, even if it was pushing beyond what was right. Raine would never understand her need to reach out for all the moments remaining.

This man intrigued her, for he was a living contradiction. He was both fierce and benevolent, like a warrior priest. And though he claimed to be a Norman loyal to King Henry, she knew he was a man of secrets.

His skin was warm beneath her fingertips, his face revealing hard planes. A sudden heat rushed through her as she explored his features. During her life, she'd never had the opportunity to be courted by a man, and her illness had shut her away from the world. Her father had isolated her until it seemed that only the hand of Death was waiting in her future.

Perhaps it was the lack of time that made her act with boldness. Or perhaps it was her sudden sense of unfairness. There was a handsome man beside her, one who attracted her in ways she didn't understand. Being so near to him was forbidden…and undeniably exciting. Why shouldn't she seize the opportunity that was before her?

Her pulse was racing, and the proximity of his body against hers was a very different kind of risk.

He leaned down and, against her lips, he murmured, "Don't move." The heat of his breath and the danger of discovery only heightened the blood racing through her. She was aware of every line of his body, of his warm hands around her, and the feeling of his hips pressed to her own.

Her imagination revelled in what it would be like to be kissed by this man. His mouth was so close to hers…and if she lifted her lips, they would be upon his.

*Don't miss*
*WARRIOR OF FIRE by Michelle Willingham.*
*Available December 2015 wherever*
*Harlequin® Historical books and ebooks are sold.*

www.Harlequin.com

# THE WORLD IS BETTER WITH

## *Romance*

Harlequin has everything from contemporary, passionate and heartwarming to suspenseful and inspirational stories.

Whatever your mood, we have a romance just for you!

Connect with us to find your next great read, special offers and more.